T0165530

EAGLE'S ECLIPSE

EAGLE'S ECLIPSE

AMERICA BEFORE COLUMBUS

JEFFREY UNDERWOOD
AND
KATE TAYLOR

iUniverse, Inc.
Bloomington

EAGLE'S ECLIPSE
America Before Columbus

Copyright © 2012 by Jeffrey Underwood and Kate Taylor.

All rights reserved. No part of this book may be used or reproduced by any means, graphic, electronic, or mechanical, including photocopying, recording, taping or by any information storage retrieval system without the written permission of the publisher except in the case of brief quotations embodied in critical articles and reviews.

iUniverse books may be ordered through booksellers or by contacting:

iUniverse
1663 Liberty Drive
Bloomington, IN 47403
www.iuniverse.com
1-800-Authors (1-800-288-4677)

Because of the dynamic nature of the Internet, any web addresses or links contained in this book may have changed since publication and may no longer be valid. The views expressed in this work are solely those of the author and do not necessarily reflect the views of the publisher, and the publisher hereby disclaims any responsibility for them.

Any people depicted in stock imagery provided by Thinkstock are models, and such images are being used for illustrative purposes only.
Certain stock imagery © Thinkstock.

ISBN: 978-1-4759-5235-3 (sc)
ISBN: 978-1-4759-5236-0 (ebk)

Library of Congress Control Number: 2012917906

Printed in the United States of America

iUniverse rev. date: 09/27/2012

TABLE OF CONTENTS

INTRODUCTION

Christopher Columbus was not yet born and unbeknownst to any European, the massive Native American city of Cahokia was bursting at its seams with a population that rivaled the population of London. Ruled by his master, the ancient vampire entity of the Forbidden Tome, Lethal Assumed and Treason's Truth finds himself as chieftain of this very city.

The tale of Kakeobuk, wise chieftain of the Mississippian Indian Mound Builders, is a lusty story of intrigue, intimate acts and emotions and of the ultimate disappearance of one and all from the face of the earth in Cahokia.

A factual picture of ancient Native American culture is painted in this tome. Indian life flows naturally and realistically throughout the saga here. The issues that the characters deal with are often huge and overwhelming. Should young virgin Indian maidens be sacrificed to their Gods as has been the perpetual tradition? Or should this cruel bloodletting to unseen supernatural beings be stopped?

Associates of the entity follow him to 1400s North America from the Scotland of Treason's Truth. And these amazingly complex vampires have unfinished stories of their own to complete.

What causes the actual collapse of the Mound Builders capital of Cahokia? Is it angry gods? Is it catastrophic natural disasters or climate change? Or is it overworking of the land and its resources. What truly would cause the total emptying and disappearance of a once thriving Indian metropolis?

Come see the tapestry woven between the covers of Eagle's Eclipse. It builds into a fabric of elegant colors, clear answers, and bawdy but loving moments, a shaman's search, a hunter's prayer, the sweetest notions of the origins of their precious corn and odes to one another that will move your heart.

The drumbeat of the gods is ever-present here. Listen to these sounds and allow them to captivate you.

Then, with a rush, let this tale sink its teeth into you.

NOT FOR EIGHTEEN
AND YOUNGER

Acknowledgments

The Blend of Jeff and Kate's Interweaving Is A Blessing

Also, Thank You For Your Character Inspiration:
Rose Smith
Ellie Mackay

Our Families For Loving Us and Understanding the Spice.

To the Lost City of Cahokia Which Was Thrilling In All of Its Truth.

To All Lost Cultures Which Fascinate Kate and Jeff No End.

To the sweetest entity and his master, whose openings in the
darkness of the spirit let the moon beams shine through

Finally, our heartfelt appreciation to all those
who make authoring a book accessible and possible.

So thank you iUniverse and Your Gracious and Talented Staff.

CHAPTER 1

DART OF SENSATION

He grunted, fell to his bare knees into the dry earth, which created a puff of quickly dispersed dust, and clutched at his ribs. He pressed long, thick and brown fingers into the area of pain and disturbance. Instantly though, he gathered his equilibrium and stood slowly as he continued to seek for anything residual. The dart of sensation had disappeared as abruptly as it had appeared.

Those surrounding him in the nearly seeded field had frozen upon seeing their Great Eagle stunned and paralyzed but then they relaxed slightly as he arose of his own accord to his customary height. It was as if he had never paused. Only his automatically probing fingers, which still roved over his ribs, gave the ruse to anyone's notion that nothing had transpired.

As if without regard, he waved his concerned compatriots back to what had been their preoccupation with the planting of maize seed into the just hoed land. The initiation of placing kernels into several inches of turned dirt was so excruciatingly crucial that their revered leader, who had come down from his luxurious structure upon the towering mound above them, was overseeing the process. His skill in laying down the tight hard nubs of corn into the soil was superlative and demonstrated his concern for the staple by which his people principally survived. He very well might have been dabbling in late hour leisurely pursuits or conjuring up ideas to turn political tasks and machinations into reality.

But he was here: roughened elbow to roughened elbow. He never shirked his people's hard work. All appreciated that. He cared; he cared for them all.

Kakeobuk stared out to the inky horizon now and then closed his eyes languidly and left them that way briefly. Behind his eyelids, his thoughts ceased wavering and he refocused easily. His eyelids separated without his willing it and he discovered a vivid clarity that he had never experienced prior to the singular moment of that flaring, vanishing pain. The pain had morphed into a sea; it was a sea that spread throughout him. He felt revived, refreshed, calm, and with a newly infused surety.

The planting proceeded beneath the warm and quiet night sky. The heat of day often was a scourge upon both people and seed. There was habitual movement through the fields, emptying of animal skin sacks filled with the precious golden kernels as those kernels were then squeezed into the loose earth. This was done purely with the aid of the light of the moon . . .

Kakeobuk seemed the same but he was utterly altered for an indeterminate amount of time.

The new essence that had just intruded here had silently groaned through nearly four hundred and fifty years in a maligned existence dwelling in a deep hole in an otherwise verdant set of Spanish hills. The agony of the wait for the arrival of his master's call was intense torture for the shade that this demon was forced to presently be.

He had his master. Otherwise, his power, potential and actual, knew almost no bounds.

The call had come unexpectedly, as was so typical, and this had been the way of it in his habitations of Septimius, Eumann and Cinaed.

He had such pent up and violent energy as he exited his hole. He was to re-inhabit a human body and take his place in the forward climb of civilization's journey.

He had been ecstatic as he shot to the dark and murky heavens above. His glee and fervor were so intense that he did not even take his despised bat form as he had while seeking out Eumann and then Cinaed.

He was an engine of concentrated speed, shapeless and rife with anticipation. This flight of his was long in miles yet brief in time. He traversed the Pacific Ocean and a third of the North American continent continuing to flow west.

Peripherally, he noticed the drier and overwrought lands cultivated below him. That was information stored for later use. His master forced him onward and downward with an invisible hand. Dart, stone shot, he was both and exploded toward the tall, tan skinned individual rapidly filling his vision. Instantaneously, he merged with this person and then became the very soul of this person.

His master was pleased.

He was now Kakeobuk and the prior Kakeobuk became subjugated and lesser.

The entity understood much immediately about the skin and the skin's culture that he had now taken over. This was the Indian's elite ruler who he now reposed within. He was unusually tall for this tribe of people. Most were of short stature. He towered over his kith, kin and subjects. He was of raven colored long hair tied in a very tight tail that was clasped with many thin copper rings to hold the hair in place. No other male had hair in his fashion. Many men and women had bangs at their forehead but not he.

This Indian was not in his dwelling presently but was aiding his community in their planting of maize that was essential for their sustenance and survival. He did not simply rule, he participated as a true leader should.

Other leaders past had let the fields be over used and these wayward acts had necessitated urgency now. Those earlier leaders would have been content to have slept the night through in their sumptuous surroundings of a very large, ornately decorated rectangular wood, thatch and mud structure built on the highest flat topped mound for near absolute protection.

Those casual chiefs would have been wrapped in luxurious animal skins and would have displayed no concern for the success of the fields as they dreamt of other issues.

Not so for the sagacious Kakeobuk.

Yet he was now to be industrious only as the sun hid below the horizon.

CHAPTER 2

ROUND MOUNDS

Kakeobuk recalled back to when he had been Eumann. A hidden, dark chamber had been difficult to find then and had been fortuitously located with Catrione's loving assistance. Here it was to be easy in that regard. The flat topped mounds of his tribe were for lavish homes; homes of their leaders and priests. But the round and conical mounds were their site of disposal and burial of the many corpses of natural or unnatural demise.

As The Great Eagle, he was planning on taking one of these hills of burial for his own. He was, after all, able to confiscate whatever he wished as their leader. He was that powerful. His mother had brought him into this position and he aimed to hold it without doubt. He was deemed a god of sorts and was embraced in awe and worship.

And so he took one. And it became his daylight tomb. No coffin was necessary either. With arms crossed over his chest, he simply reclined upon any level surface in the always midnight chamber. Oil lamps routinely lit these dugouts but he had the sight of a vampire now and required no such device. His vision in shadow was better than a mortal's in the light of the hard shining sun.

His distinctiveness of height and power was not the only unique facet that pulled on his life. This other was something that did not favor him. It was an aspect in a leader's life that, at his age, he should have acquired previously. He was determined to have it soon.

He was already into his mid-twenties and he had no bride as of yet. He was vigorously sought after; he had taken many maidens to their deflowering already but had not discovered his heart's desire. Many stoked his passion but not one had stirred and enflamed his always seeking heart. With the entity inside him, he comprehended why that had been.

Kakeobuk remembered back to a period of shared bliss with a woman of Dal Riata descent. He had blocked her vision of him all the while that he had been a formless, shapeless wraith. There could be no succor between them then. Now he was flesh. And she was who he would have.

He was no longer willing to wait anymore. He had waited five and a half centuries; an eternity to most.

He recollected their substance as they had entwined gorgeously with one another long ago. To this date, except for his master, he had been slave to no creation upon earth. And then, as a mature Cinaed, he had become her slave. He had not realized until then that he had a yearning heart; a heart that did more than lust. A bit of Catrione and then all of Aiobheean imprisoned him amongst his beating emotions. He loved this Aiobheean so and would have her again without one shred of doubt about it.

What picture did this particular beauty paint for him? She was not a member of his chiefdom as she was tall, lithesome, pale, and of long strawberry blond hair. She was the polar opposite of the look of the Cahokia women.

His mind demanded that he paint more of a picture of her now. He was powerless to do otherwise!

She was a magnificent beauty who surpassed the many magnificent beauties of her time and culture.

Her lengthy locks and soft curls had a fine sheen and bright luster.

Her skin was smooth so as to make him ache to put his fingers gently to her cheeks. Those cheeks wonder was alabaster-like in its creamy evenness.

As if pinched to a rosy hue, her cheeks offset the porcelain surface of her face so strongly that her few freckles were barely noticed.

Her eyes were softly washed over in an aquamarine blue with flecks of emerald and gold.

And in the middle of this radiance was a set of full lips in a startlingly vivid raspberry color.

She was the bearer of exquisitely full and round breasts that thrust forward even when she did not desire them to. She was hugely bounteous there and yet these breasts hung perfectly; high yet wonderfully pendulous as well. Her aureoles and nipples had the same raspberry stain as her lips. These aureoles were small but her nipples were very thick and sensitive.

Her belly had the tiniest bit of curve; that feature was so very feminine.

Finally, her legs were lean and supple. She had been pleased at their shape and subtly muscled tone.

His cock swelled in memory and began to nudge the material at his groin up and aside. He was fortunate that it was dark and all the other planters were concentrating on their task. It was deemed unmanly to erect in public.

He took his long and wide shaft, pipes of veins exhibited, in hand though. He bent over so that he was low to the ground and less visible. He had to stroke his manhood hard and fast right then! He did not care the shame it might bring him if he was caught; especially as their leader. Her delightful remembrance compelled him to do this above all else.

He stifled his urge to growl and gasp as spurts drove violently into the soil. He had bent his organ firmly downward so that these spurts would be unseen. That made his ejaculation even more powerful as more blood was trapped in his surging cock. He was bigger than he ever recalled.

He spilled his seed then as he planted the seed of the golden other.

CHAPTER 3

AIOBHEEAN ALONE

S he had erupted from the King's window at Scone Abbey so long ago. She had fled incestuous evil that had annihilated her love for her liege lord, her husband and the man who was the father of her children. Her vast wings had shattered the calm of the night sky as she had labored to find solitude in her bereft frame of mind.

Her bruised spirit had gradually eased its terrible grip on her fluttering heart. Eventually, she was capable of coherent thought, a regular rhythm of her heart that no longer twitched or pounded in a raucous drumbeat; she had found her breath and had recaptured her imperiled dignity.

She remained close to her children and followed that by doing the same for succeeding generations of her offspring. If, as she reckoned, it took approximately twenty years to spawn a new generation, then she had observed nearly two dozen generations appear before her ever watchful eyes. Constantine was almost a faded memory for her. Truly, when she closed her eyes to imagine her first born son's face, she was not able to conjure up even a single facial characteristic.

A tear leaked from between her clenched eyelids as this realization just now had struck home for her.

Her family had become so dilute presently.

She had also undergone the shifts that Scotland had suffered since the brief era of reigning supreme alongside Cinaed. This country's borders had expanded and contracted continuously. Its independence had come, gone and returned as warriors fought ceaselessly with the treasure of red blood saturating the terrain.

She drank often of that selfsame blood that was so constantly spilled. Yet, in some deep inner chamber of herself, she loathed that she was captive to the undead ritual that kept her feeding, supping, dining, draining and leaching the crimson life force from her many victims for her own damnable primal needs.

Aiobheean had been alone all of this half millennium. It was too much. She began to sob in her anguish and to let her guard down within that welter of emotions.

She had fiercely fought off Cinaed's attempts to find her. She desired no further part of enjoining with him.

Since she was privy now to the fact that Cinaed had been inhabited when she cherished him and their lives most, she reasoned that she must have felt a pull toward that demonic essence that had abandoned Cinaed.

She had sensed a tug upon her only moments ago as she wept; a weeping whose sobs suddenly collapsed and she became utterly silent, attuned and vigilant. Animation and excitement stirred. And it was not provoked by her children whatsoever. No, this was an altogether different excitement for her. This was a sensation that had been absent so long. A seed of passion had found its way inside her with that tug. And this emotion was one that she had cherished once and most certainly would again.

There were more of these tugs and with each her heart pounded and her fount moistened.

She swooned a bit and these tugs of hers swept her into its slipstream. Her heart followed it, her spirit followed it, her lustrous form converted into the beating of a bat's wings and she lost all powers of restraint; she followed it with every fiber within her.

She flew to a destination of mystery and total unfamiliarity.

Had her entity found human form? Was this his call to her then?

This was her joy and profound hope!

The swoon and swirl surrounding her automatic motion vanished. She shape shifted and was winged no more. She touched ground.

Her bare feet bore the dry, slightly burning sensation of hot and packed earth under her soles. The soil was baked, the air was still and warm and yet it was moon time with shadows of great length covering all things. Her sight sharpened more so and she scrutinized her surroundings. She was at the very perimeter of a just seasoned and prepared field where bent individuals garnished the ground with seed.

She scanned and wondered as to who would be her lover now?

In that instant, he spun towards her. She saw the mixed look of some surprise and much tenderness upon his countenance. She even noticed her pale, ghostly reflection upon his amber irises.

This man rose above her somewhat. He was gaunt yet his entire body was a canvas of ripped muscle. He was also practically nude and his skin was a light tan. He had no mustache or beard; his hair was pitch black and pulled back. This included ashen eyebrows, a ledge of thick lashes and a lengthy tail of hair that was ringed with shining bands of a reddish-brown metal. This tail hung over his shoulder, as it had whipped there in his quick earlier movement, and hung down to his belly. He wore only a rectangular animal hide loin cloth and a small seed sack.

He bore no tattoos whatsoever.

The outline of his cock dented the hide and gave a whisper of a vast soft shaft hanging beneath. His softness changed abruptly in her sudden fantasy; a fantasy where he placed his huge hard shaft into her drenched vault and then thrust deep into her until they came together.

Her cleft throbbed so.

She was utterly engulfed by him. It was her entity and her lover.

CHAPTER 4

FIST IN GLOVE

He strode in her direction and quickly placed his arm around her shoulders. She immediately leaned into him as if she was a canoe finding safe harbor. Kakeobuk signaled to his surprised, then stunned, onlookers to settle back into their prior endeavors.

Row upon row of earnestly working Cahokia Indians hushed but had to stare as subtly as possible. They had never witnessed a female who appeared as this woman did. There was a mixed sensation of awe and fright at Aiobheean's difference. That she walked as they did seemed their only similarity. Her delicacy of all but her brazen bust, her lean height, her pale, pale skin and cascading blonde locks hammered at their threshold of believability. They were unable to see her eye color but collectively guessed that they were anything but brown. And they would have been so absolutely correct!

Kakeobuk sheltered this alien woman as best as he could with his body, then he guided her to what would become their mound of repose. He desired her at length and so took her where he and she were protected from natural light all of the day long.

He was ecstatic at her presence and, though he had just ejaculated immensely moments ago, was not capable of remaining soft as they neared the mound. She was incapable of resisting her impulses towards him as well.

As they receded into the pitched shadows, she reached for his prominently exposed shaft and stroked it hard and slow with her fist. He moaned ever so slightly, as did she. She squeezed his huge erection with all the strength in that fist that she was able to muster and milked him deliciously. He was quivering and his cockhead was now bulbous, almost purple and draining beads of dew for her.

He was embarrassed at his excitement but would have succumbed to the pleasure ultimately.

As he pulled the wood woven sodden door of his mound open, her hand remained clutched to his enormous shaft. The paradox of his outsize organ was that the fleshy give of the exterior was supported underneath by the steel of his desire for her. His cock was an extended fist in a velvet glove. And she loved that!

She had been no one's lover since escaping Scone on that intensely traumatic eve. She had found her shelter after in the lower elevations of Am Monadh. Holes and caves dotted that landscape profusely. She had hidden and did not open herself up to any feeling other than those of alert pride as her clan produced and then reproduced. That was a breathtaking pleasure for her.

This was the first of a breathtaking pleasure of a different kind! And it was vibrant and lush. The floodgates of her pent up libidinous energy streamed out of her with Kakeobuk. He was the entity and she was his!

Both were undead and saw clearly in the gloom of the mounds interior.

His mind drifted for a moment as it was perpetually active. This burial mound was not yet cleared of human debris of bones and rotting flesh. The burial mound, as was typical, was stacked with the corpses of those beautiful native women chosen for ritual sacrifice to appease their Eagle God. The winged god, Wahkakiya, was so powerful that he ruled over the mighty sun, moon, earth, sky and corn gods combined. Wahkakiya was man and bird so that he swept over the Earth by ground and air when not supporting the universe upon his shoulders.

Kakeobuk felt himself, all vampires, to be Wahkakiya. The human face of the Eagle God should bear his countenance therefore; making him master of infinite space.

His arrogance shocked him suddenly. He dashed this rumination from his mind and returned every bit of his focus back to his ever love.

Soon this chamber was to be emptied of all indications of human death and would contain only a setup where a taut leather bottom layer, piled over by an abundance of animal hides and furs, would be supported by four thick hewn wooden legs. Notches were cut into each leg at the perfect level so that the strong leather thongs lashed to both the taut hide and each leg would hold and never move.

For now, the decaying hills of flesh were to be left alone until the pairs desires were quenched he surmised.

Aiobheean balked for a brief instant. She may have been eternal and ungodly but she was not at all eager to cavort amongst such repulsive surroundings. Her paralysis as she scanned the area sent a very clear message to Kakeobuk. Simultaneously, they lost their enchantment with lovemaking. And it was even more frustrating for him as they were not adept yet at speaking words out loud with one another. He had to teach her the language and he had to do it immediately. Mind talk just did not satisfy as actual words did.

He embarked upon an action that he had never done before as he had never prized any being as he prized Aiobheean. He had special capacities as a vampire that she did not and she would never have. He spoke the tongue of the individual that he fused with instantaneously. She had to learn the tongue as any human had to. Could he give her a capacity, as he possessed, without laboring over the slow absorption of the mechanics of Cahokia speech? He thought so.

He sent a shred of his shapeless essence to her.

She experienced the dart that Kakeobuk had earlier that night. Hers was barely painful as she had been gifted only a small fraction of the entire spirit that Kakeobuk had received.

It was enough! She spoke aloud to him in the native tongue here and said, "I have trembled for this moment with you. Yet we must find circumstances that allow the effect that our love deserves.

"That is not here now!"

Kakeobuk understood even before she had finished her first sentence that their love demanded particular consideration of ambiance, care and concern.

He was also impressed that her gracious and exceptional style remained wherever she found herself.

"I love your clear and correct sentiments. And I love you."

The next step for them was for him to take her to his royal quarters, postpone the lovemaking that they both wished for, clear this mound quickly, return her here to rest the required undead sleep and then introduce her to the city with an Indian name. They were sure to cherish her.

CHAPTER 5

TRIO'S TREK

C inaed awoke from an outrageous dream of his and Aiobheean's fierce and passionate entwining. He sat up so rapidly that he lost his equilibrium briefly and his shelter spun sickeningly. Once that cleared, he was amazed at his good fortune.

Aiobheean's whereabouts was revealed to him. She must have inadvertently forgotten to block him and he was now privy to all that he had desperately craved for nigh on to an eternity. Or, at least, it had felt so to him.

He, Catrione and Eumann had remained within the fluctuating borders of Scotland on a hunch that his long lost Queen would stay near their children and progeny. He had been deeply mistaken. Or had she just changed locations?

He was so excited that he stomped on his guesswork and saw that she was in a far flung country of once rich fields and luxuriant pastures. The land currently had a dusty and slightly barren appearance. He was also intensely shocked at how hot and bright the sun was there! This seemed an anathema to a vampire but nighttime occurred there as it did anywhere.

How had she chosen this terrain though? It must have had to do with the ultimate entity who had resided within Eumann and Cinaed a while. There was no vision there. The fiend obviously prevented their undead seer sight from penetrating his barriers. This entity was so much stronger than they.

No matter as he comprehended where the heart was; the heart that he must recapture.

Catrione spoke to her son then, "Cinaed, let us go there now. We all see what you see. And we are ready as you are!"

"It is the opportune moment, Cinaed. Let us three fly there." Eumann was adamant.

Upon their departure from the British Isles, night had reappeared once again since Kakeobuk and Aiobheean had reunited. The field had been fully laden with maize seed and the area brimming with Cahokia life twenty four hours before was empty and stone silent as the trio's trek came to an easy end.

Cinaed quickly bored into the brain of one of the sleeping residents. He was probing in order to assign appropriate names for each of them. His probing managed names but not speech. Speech was to be a learning process for them all unless they were as fortunate as Aiobheean.

Cinaed, Catrione and Eumann departed their prior Scottish appellations without reserve or regret.

"Eumann, you are Mahkwa. Repeat it over and over until it is reflexive when you say it. It means Moon Bear and fits you well. Use it wisely.

"Mother, you now become Ashkipaki. I love your emerald eyes. And that means exactly that.

"I am Mikilenia. Winged Man feels suitable for me." Cinaed smiled at this.

The others nodded their heads in assent and murmured their new names to themselves.

Mahkwa swiveled to scan the city that they found themselves ensconced in. All three looked in awe at the massive fields and structures surrounding and dwarfing them.

Here is what they discerned about Cahokia as they stealthily paced through what most surely was abuzz with activity when the sun held sway.

They peered upward at a landscape bombarded with very large prominences. Upon the crown of many of these mounts, homes and temples were built. All temples and some homes exuded a luxury that was beyond all of the other structures. The most lavishly decorated of these stood atop the hills with highest elevation. And then, peculiarly, a few of these peaks were not flat and held no structures upon them at all.

They now were surrounded by the dirt monstrosities, yet were positioned upon and viewed a level area that appeared to be a commons for the citizenry; a plaza they thought. It was enormous as this entire city seemed to be.

They quietly padded through a low slung arched wood tunnel that led to an area that must have been a playfield. The surface was of packed sand and was incredibly smooth. A tall post existed upon a rise at the precise center of the arena. Nothing was placed upon this pole but other less prominent poles at the perimeter; those poles had several still decaying decapitated heads speared in place at their upper end.

The trio knew barbarism surrounded them as it had in Scotland too.

What the three were actually seeking was a shelter from the sun in the morning. They needed to be secure by then or face an eternal demise that would be swift and absolute. The harshness of the possibility made all vampires tremble.

They were wholly unobserved by the guards spaced equidistant from one another at several platforms built into the wood wall that was the perimeter palisades of the city. The palisades separated the core of the city from the fields organized beyond the wooden wall with its singular gate. This stockade was at least double their height and was created from many thousands of logs that had slender limbs interwoven log to log and then a layer of packed mud thrown over the entire wood edifice. The mud had peeled from several locations and that is how the three comprehended its full configuration.

This city was erected on an earthen elevation with further elevations scooped onto the original elevation. It was ingenious in that the entire formation of the city served to protect the integrity of continuing and safe Indian life here.

Mikilenia walked them to one of the rounded mounds. He was almost in a frenzy to find and confront his Aiobheean. He felt her presence behind the door to the interior of this mound. He knew that when he flung the door open, two of their problems would be solved. Aiobheean was there and so was their protection from any burning rays thrust at them by dawn's arrival.

He almost tore the door from its fasteners and the three of them rushed into the cavernous space.

CHAPTER 6

DRUMBEAT OF THE GODS

The air wafting about their special hillock was now filled with the stench of rotting flesh as Kakeobuk had, in his haste, simply moved the crumbling bodies to an open pit proximate to the mound. In order to make the air more palatable for their mingled breathing inside, a weed known as oyka was burned continuously. The smoke emitted had its own musky odor tinged with a scent of cinnamon. The smoke was allowed to settle upward and the cinnamon scent clung to the earthen walls and transformed the atmosphere surrounding them into an aroma that was warm and sweet.

Kakeobuk cradled his treasure, now content with her new name of Minkitooni, in his strong left arm and asked for privacy for him and her. Mikilenia scowled and raised an eyebrow as he barely acquiesced. Mahkwa and Ashkipaki bowed their heads in silence as they retreated to another darkened chamber in the large cavernous space.

Kakeobuk had taken Minkitooni by the hand and led her into their personal hollow. It was night black there but both scoured out the details of the area as they were enveloped by a cloak of impenetrable shadows. The undead pair shrank into the gloom and paid no heed to the others soon enough.

The wood and leather platform that was large enough to accommodate Kakeobuk and Minkitooni filled their portion of the mound's interior. The hide of the deer had been dressed, scraped and soaked in a fermented mashed corn liquid, producing this soft as butter, bed on stilts.

The aroma of this leather bed was warm, sweet and a bit biting. The surface of the leather was cool to touch like the chamber itself. When skin was exposed to the platform's surface, it would heat the leather and provide a cushion where rest and now pleasure would be had.

Before taking to the bed, Kakeobuk invited Minkitooni to share in a ritual that would celebrate their soon to be mingled and joining flesh.

To the side, in a small corner of their area, there was a simple set of items which the couple would use in ceremony to celebrate the sensuality that they sought in the uniting of their bodies.

Comb from the bees had been collected and cut into bite size pieces. Kakeobuk took a piece of the honeycomb and raised it up, nodding to Minkitooni. He invited her to close her eyes. She did so and Kakeobuk began touching her in the nooks of her body that held the drumbeats of the gods. He did so to awaken the sacred forces and call on the divine powers to build the pulse within her and give her ease of accepting his now swelling and hot heated member.

He touched the waxen sweet comb to the right side of her neck, her wrists, and the crook of her elbow where the blue palpitating vein steadily throbbed. He gently grasped her foot and pressed the honeycomb into her instep and followed up her leg, to her torso where he lifted her pendulous breast that he so longed to kiss, and depressed the comb into her flesh there, making the honey ooze from the wax and drip down her soft and pale skin.

Minkitooni, felt the sweetness warm her when Kakeobuk had finished painting the golden dew upon her. She felt the drumbeats of her pulse increase and she heard it in her ears as the blood coursed through her, more forcefully now. Her breathing quickened with the honeyed blessing on her flesh.

He took the piece of the comb into his mouth and chewed its sweetness. He craved tasting the honey from her flesh. He offered her a cube of the honeyed wax; she licked her lips where a drop of honey clung and he heard her as she throatily murmured, "Mmmmm."

Kakeobuk next offered a small empty pottery cup to Minkitooni. He then raised an earthen vessel and poured the liquid tiswin, ale made from the fermented corn, into her cup. As tradition had it, he sipped the liquid first and offered it to her. She poured the tiswin for him, sipped it and offered it back to him. This ritual was complete now and marked the important joining of the chieftain with his love, Minkitooni.

Kakeobuk rose and assisted his love to her feet. He began to hum and took her hands in his, moving his body so close to her that not a single husked leaf from the corn would fit between the two of them. He moved back and forth in a dance that provided enough friction to his cock under the thin leather loincloth to cause it to build, lengthen and thicken. Minkitooni felt it too, and rubbed her fount against his manhood as she moaned very low, like the purr of the contented brush cat.

She deftly removed her thin sheath of covering; she desired his touch intensively.

His hands left her hands as he rubbed his palms on her pendulous breasts. The nipples and aureoles puckered under his touch, causing them to burgeon, and she tipped her head back in fraught pleasure. His cock was working its magic upon her and she trembled with heat for more of him.

Kakeobuk began kissing her honeyed points. He licked her neck and grazed his teeth there, knowing that he could slice through flesh with his razor sharp fangs. He kept those fangs in check now, not wanting to find any blood from his love. She was already turned and responded to his fluid efforts so sensuously. Every time he licked, suckled and nibbled at a pulse point, Minkitooni swooned more and her moans became more audible.

At the same time that Kakeobuk was performing erotically upon Minkitooni, Mikilenia, Mahkwa, and Ashkipaki were in a removed area where the voices and sounds of Kakeobuk and Minkitooni carried clearly to them. Mikilenia snarled in a muted fashion deep within his throat, yet was unable to resist listening intently to the patently loving sounds emitted from his once cherished Queen.

Under his own trews, his cock began to swell, no matter how he tried to stifle its growth. Ashkipaki was stirred herself and wanted to kiss Mahkwa, who resisted in front of Mikilenia. He did not want to cause any more disturbances to Mikilenia's already pained mind nor potentially arouse Mikilenia regarding his mother again.

Kakeobuk carried Minkitooni to the leather bed. He placed her gently on its surface. The backs of her hands found its soft giving surface and she moved about to feel it all over as it warmed to meet her body temperature.

After removing his tented loincloth, Kakeobuk joined her on the bed. It was taut but had enough give to draw them both to its center, as if it called to them to unite.

Kakeobuk continued to kiss all the honey sweetened pulse points. Minkitooni was amazed at how pleasurable his kisses were at her wrist and the crook of her elbow. Every kiss and lick that Kakeobuk planted there went straight to her now fiery hot core. He sweetened her nipples with his kisses, but it was under her left breast that Kakeobuk knew where the strongest drumbeat of the gods was; right there. Minkitooni arched her back and held his head so he would not move from that spot. She moaned at the heat his kissing and suckling there brought to her fount; the ember of her crown jewel was shooting sensual sparks that imprisoned her within her desire for him.

He reached down and was able to take hold of one more piece of honeycomb. He moved lower and found himself between Minkitooni's long beautiful legs. Seeking out the hard kernel, the shiny glowing seed of red maize, the jewel buried within her center, he found it protruding and he squeezed the honey onto her there. He used his tanned fingers to rub the honey all around her taut kernel and into her glistening opening as well. He breathed his warm breath on her and she raised her hips, trying to find the mouth that blew the tantalizing breath onto her.

He separated her nether lips and gently licked the honey from her. Then he used his almost magical tongue to focus all his attention upon her clitoris. The kernel began to grow from the fleshly earth where it was planted. It swelled out of its hood and begged for him to taste and lick. He obliged her but would not let her come to her climax yet. He knew her drumbeats were loud and forceful when he was with her and they lushly delivered the music of the drums to each other.

His bulbous organ, the cockhead swollen and filled with blood, grew even more when Minkitooni grasped it hard and squeezed. The glistening pearly fluid at the tip was oozing out of the opening. Kakeobuk took the last of the honeycomb and mashed it, letting the honey mix with his own drops of creamy liquid. Minkitooni used her thumb to spread it all around. She moaned again and pulled him on top of her as she was so ready to receive him. Honey sweet and slick, Kakeobuk entered her, filling her up with his erect and heavy cock. He stayed still for a moment to let them enjoy the union they had waited so long for.

He kissed her deeply. She trembled then and Kakeobuk felt the tiny drops of tears that had already formed at the outside corner of her eyes. He brushed them away with his thumbs and held her face in his hands.

"Please," she whispered. "Please. You know what it is that I crave and need. I need you now".

"Yessss," Kakeobuk hissed in raw pleasure as he began the thrusting that would take them to the edge in flight and back.

Once again with his love, he was equally one again with his love. Thrusting! Thrusting! They moved together in unison. They had sought this for so long!

It was hot breath panted past one another's cheeks. It was skin to skin and touch to touch.

Moving harder, faster, quickening and getting closer and closer, it was pain and pleasure in one.

The insistent godly drumbeats, louder and louder inside them, shook them. The sounds occurred in unison; reaching the crescendo of nature's music, ready now to . . . .

The climax of their lovemaking overtook them in a union of their senses. Together they saw the white light of the starburst within them. They tasted and smelled the honey and cinnamon that had washed over them. They cried together aloud as the spasms rocked them. The sensations and vibrations erupted as her pulsing and contracting milked the cream from Kakeobuk that filled the once empty well of Minkitooni. She was complete now. He was satiated; delighted to the utmost.

Oh, the drumbeats of the gods, they were happy sounds.

Kakeobuk and Minkitooni had found their precious love again.

Mikilenia had not.

CHAPTER 7

BLACK RAVEN'S VIEW

She failed to comprehend why the torches were lit and the game was being played an hour after sunset. It was so much more difficult to make out the stone and stick play of the warrior's engaged in Tchungkee combat via the flickering light of the torch. Possibly it was much cooler and that Kakeobuk was taking mercy on the laboring participants. Their chieftain had dictated the time of play and one did not defy one's leader.

She did chafe at that lesson on occasion.

Anteekwa was engrossed in the performance before her in spite of her questions regarding Kakeobuk's choices. He had been of a strange nature the last several days. She had noticed that he did not leave his dwelling anymore between sunrise and sunset. He spent more time in his burial mound than he did in his abode upon another massive mound that was also his. He was accompanied by creatures, human she surmised, but like no humans that she had ever viewed before.

Black Raven, Anteekwa, was gifted in so many ways. She was astute, very, very observant and was also determined to make her mark on the terribly shrunken city of Cahokia. It had once been a city of so much command that none questioned its right to rule vast tracts of land surrounding it. Now it was a city where the revered game of Tchungkee was played in the near dark and her chieftain consorted with individuals of an image that was not Indian or even similar.

He had enclosed himself with one female who had Princess Anteekwa's appearance slightly. But even she seemed to ally herself with one of the alien males, not even Kakeobuk. And then there was another alien male who repulsed and fascinated her simultaneously. How could this be? But it was! He had a feral gleam to his eyes that the others had lesser of. He was chiseled muscularly and large. She was not used to large men. Kakeobuk had been one of the few tall men roving the city. And even he was lean, not compact and fiercely defined like the one she repeatedly glanced at. She loved his tattoos the best amongst them all besides.

The worst of it though was that Kakeobuk, who was one of her uncles, stood side by side with a female who was sickly pale, lean to dimensions that were frightening to Anteekwa, with long and thick blond hair that glowed in the shadows and a bust larger than her own by a fraction. She did not countenance that easily. She was used to catching vast attention for her own large jut there. No woman had matched her in that regard in the entire city until now. And now there were two others; but did the one count?

Against her better instincts, she did count that one because she was able to identify with her a bit. The other, the wraith, was simply unbelievable and not worthy of her cousin's consideration.

They must be Indian for they wore clothes resembling her own. But of what city and tribe were they from? Of that she had no remote idea.

Had they been dressed by Kakeobuk? She wondered that suddenly.

In the meantime, she brought her attention back to the spirited game at hand before her on the playfield. Tchungkee was a game of such epic skill to her. She was not allowed to play it herself as no women were. But she reveled in the abilities of the various men of the city who participated.

The contestants practiced in all of their free moments at honing their skills so that they were able to constantly best one another.

She marveled at their adeptness at handling the round stone disks that were very heavy to begin with. And then their strength as they rolled the stones on their sides far over the hard sanded surface. What fascinated her most was the wicked accuracy of the participant warriors throw of their long sticks as the rock rolled to a stop. Whose stick would land nearest the stone as it ceased motion?

These skills applied here and on the battlefield. The game was revered in this city and had long ago been shown to and adopted by the other cities that spread along the great rivers that sped past their city of Cahokia.

Eagle Priest, Kakeokoke, another of her uncles, stood side by side with Anteekwa. She glanced at him and he remained utterly still and without reaction to the game of any kind. He was shaman-priest and she knew that it was immodest if he responded in any manner to the excitement on the playfield. She comprehended, though, that were she to ask him a direct question, he would answer her immediately and honestly.

"How do you respond to the strange and sudden visitors surrounding Kakeobuk?"

"He is wise and our chieftain. He is the savior of the land as well. I trust his judgment without hesitation. He is my brother and he has never ceased to impress me."

"And what do you think of the pallid woman sheltered by him? Do you not find her and her companions worrisome?"

"He will ask me for signs if he feels that necessary. Then and only then will I concern myself. And I will report the divinations to him and follow them myself."

Anteekwa resigned herself to this being all that her uncle would say as he had now crossed his arms over his chest and stood resolute!

Her misgivings were sharp and distinct and she was not about to let them go with the simple notion that her uncle, Kakeobuk, was privy to some special knowledge that she and the others of the tribe did not have.

Kakeokoke assessed the situation thoroughly and without another word spoken. His beautiful niece was someone he loved and cherished deeply. Yet she was also riddled by headstrong impulses that were nearly impossible to quell. If it had been that she was only headstrong it would not have been a significant problem. But she was incredibly stubborn as well. Once she struck upon a notion, that notion lingered seemingly forever.

And she had a capacity to manipulate others easily in addition. She did this with her womanly guile and appearance if words were not enough to persuade another. Her pendulous curves and ungodly beauty were supremely potent enticements and allures to men in particular!

He would watch her closely in regards to his brother's newly acquired acquaintances.

CHAPTER 8

UNRESTRAINED DESIRE

M ikilenia was only mildly interested in the game proceeding before him. He, his mother and Mahkwa remained engaged only to the degree needed to appear involved and interested. This was principally for the sake of the crowd assembled for the Tchungkee match who were also studiously observing them as additional objects associated with their Great Eagle.

One pair of eyes amongst the rapt onlookers kept returning to repeatedly renew her assessment of him. And though Mikilenia had not yet escaped his mingled love, lust and resentment for the connection seemingly lost between Minkitooni and him, this woman, standing in proximity with an obvious spiritual servant of some importance, would yield delights almost equal to that of Minkitooni. Also she had the voluptuous appearance of his mother whom he would never tryst with again but whom he considered one of gorgeous proportions and height.

He experienced flare after flare of supremely unrestrained lust for this particular female gathered with the rest of the enthusiastic fans on the sidelines.

He had to have her! And he would have her in a fashion here and now!

His creature's mind drove its prod into her soul immediately. She danced to it throughout the game without fully understanding the blush of her unleashed sexual energy. And this while she stood almost still; supposedly captivated by the sport of the warriors but actually was the glad puppet of Mikilenia's invisible control over her.

He stripped her bare and she allowed it with a bottomless hunger for him to do exactly that to her. The reddened flush that crept up her chest to her throat and even her cheeks was, fortunately, not noticeable in an almost perfect blend with her tan colored skin. She panted softly yet subtly and slowly as if nonchalantly. She covered her soft deer hide skirt with the flat of one palm as if stunned by the player's feats. She truly wanted to feel her throb there. She was both riveted and stunned at the ferocity of her rising passion for the other across the field. She pressed herself ever so surreptitiously as her excitement doubled and then trebled.

She must have him as well!

His powers laid her exposed before him as she held her stance from afar.

And what did he see as his mind probed her full nudity that he handled as gently yet passionately as he did now? He observed her beauty in its totality. She offered it up to him but he would have taken it regardless of her initial response be it acquiescence or resistance. He was to prevail here unlike with Minkitooni! He let that thought dash out of his mind instantly. He did not want his focus to be diminished as he chose to seal his connection with the lovely stranger.

So what of her look, lines and proportions? He shifted back to his tableau swiftly and gladly! Her face was truly divine. Her forehead was nearly covered with the standard raven hued bangs, yet pearlescent shell beads were strategically tangled in those bangs. Her lean facial contours were also framed by a thick dark braid falling sweetly over each ear. She had a colorful small feather piercing the end knot of each braid. The innocent and provocative sexuality here tore at Mikilenia's heart.

He was delaying their eventual entwining, yes he was that sure, as the delicious prolongation of each and every moment with her added to the heat and ultimate frenzy of what would be their unabashed consummation. She was already such a delight! Her facial features were of eyes of huge size and a lustrous golden color; a brown with so much telltale lightness. The eyebrows were ample and magnificently sweeping over a ledge of very long black eyelashes. She possessed an aquiline nose and etched cheekbones. Her lips were robust and of a fine light red rose stain. Her smile had not been revealed to him. It would be.

She had supple and delicate curvature of throat followed in a smooth line devoid of any irregularities of skin or fold. His cock firmed to his chagrin. This probing of his to her body and soul lowered below her throat easily, languidly.

The effect of his searching her out was as if she were in a deeply held caress that would not abate. It moved her as intensely as if it were happening in the flesh.

Mikilenia had to clasp his fingers over his loin cloth as he needed to disguise his thickening and lengthening dimensions. But he was not about to stop as his demand for her was paramount. He edged behind Kakeobuk slightly; enough for disclosure of his face but not his cock.

And the richness of her figure, as he probed and caressed her more, was creating monstrous size within his minimal garb. His groin was on fire and the flame continued to consume him.

He viewed the apex of her cleavage and it pulled him into her fields of flesh there acutely. Her curves were astounding as the mounds of her city were astounding. It was also rare as many of the native maidens he had already seen were short and not excessively rounded. This woman was no taller than the females surrounding her at this very moment. But her chest was so powerfully large.

His vision had disrobed her completely but, in reality, her supple tunic was stretched to a point where her aureoles and nipples pressed in severe points against the material.

She preferred it otherwise but she aroused all the males who associated with her or even just glanced her way.

What he noted without impediment was that she was vastly curved, full and high with the tiniest of midnight black aureoles. Her nipples though were thick and long. The aureoles did not matter whatsoever in their almost vanishing. As a matter of fact, the center of her breasts appeared as entirely nipple and that was excruciatingly erotic to him. And they were so evident in their hue against the tan expanse of her breasts' abundance.

He was utterly tantalized and promptly mind-sucked upon one nipple to gauge its sensitivity. As he did this, he stared at her. Even from their distance, he caught her gasp. Luckily, it coincided with the gasp and cheer of the audience as a spear struck perfectly with the stone on the sandy surface. Equally, her tremble and slightly writhing gesture was missed by everyone but him.

He was aware that they must not find release now. That was not an act over which he was able to exert any control and so he did not seek it presently.

Tchungkee was ending. So must he. He rushed. He kissed her other nipple. He kissed over her just barely curved belly. He touched her high, small set of buttocks. He stroked her muscled and slender legs. He licked at her elongated, ruby red and slickened jewel just once. He pressed with one of his long fingers into her Venus mound's opening an instant. Then he ceased all invisible activity between them.

Anteekwa almost fell to her knees with this final delicious assault upon her. She held though as her head and body swirled profoundly.

All applauded. The match was concluded.

Their match, their game, had just begun.

CHAPTER 9

CELESTIAL CENTER

H e was Shaman and he was principal Eagle Priest. And now he had been adorned with new, very powerful, responsibilities by Great Eagle, Kakeobuk. It had stunned him a while but he was now adapting and had listened thoroughly.

That his brother was now vampire and that Kakeobuk had informed him of this had initially been terrifying. But Kakeobuk's words had ultimately been calming, detailed and wise. Kakeokoke also comprehended that it was not altogether his brother speaking to him. A force much stronger than any human being exhorted him to understand. And he was determined not only to discern but to obey the rules of leadership as dictated by the creature residing now within Kakeobuk's skin.

Light was a curse to the undead. So his chieftain required an absolutely trustworthy individual to rule the day.

Kakeobuk had already pronounced to the people of his city instantly following the last Tchungkee contest that he had a mysterious and suddenly acquired sensitivity to the sun which caused him to be weak to the point of faintness. He anointed Kakeokoke as his second then and there. Kakeokoke had been speechless as his tongue cleaved to the roof of his mouth.

After his announcement, Kakeobuk had signaled to Kakeokoke to come and parlay with him privately. This was when he was informed of all.

The city's activity did not cease simply because one person, even the august commander and chieftain, did not appear. Decisions still had to be made and carried out, daytime ceremonies had to be presided over, emergencies had to be resolved, the doings of trade happenings had to be handled and much more besides.

As a matter of fact, Kakeokoke was using the pole calendar and observing the sun's shadows to calculate the appropriate period to perform their fertility rites for the maize that had just been planted. Beans and squash were crops nearly as vital as corn too and would be well served by the ritual that must be quickly accomplished. Though the ceremony always occurred at night, the precise evening was determined by how the sun and its shadows fell upon these poles. They foretold, on an annual basis, the exact celestial center of the yellow orb in the bright turquoise sky; the period when day and night were of equal length with one another. It happened twice in a year. As one approached, planting was accomplished. As the other approached, harvesting was completed.

These poles, painted with red ochre, formed a circle. Kakeokoke knew their number and it was forty eight. They had used their universal measure to find poles of the same height once the lower end was securely dug into the ground. This same measure gave them exact specifications for the distance between the poles and from side to side of the circle standing. A pole placed perfectly in the center of the wooden configuration formed was as crucial as all the others.

He and his priests were very proud of this labor of love. It was one of several of this kind but was the most accurate of them all.

He stepped to the location for sighting and knew the shadows thrown, equal in length, indicated the next evening for watering the ground with crimson.

A maiden had already been chosen for the express purpose of honoring the goddess of corn most particularly.

The temple area was always prepared for this endeavor. Hushed anticipation blanketed the city.

Once finished with his task, he slowly wheeled in a circle of his own. He loved the people and dominion of Cahokia. He wanted to breathe it in briefly.

His image was expansive and interwoven with joy. This image combined his view inside the gated area and what he knew outside of that same area. He was inside. His ability to see the outside was blocked by the very wooden wall that kept the more significant members of the community secure.

His abode, as was Kakeobuk's when Kakeobuk desired to use it as such, was the massive temple that lay across the horizontal peak of the mound that loomed over all of the citizenry of Cahokia. Terraced stairs were hacked out of the sod that lay over the surface of the grand mound. Below this magnificent creation of hard packed dirt, stomped down by a multitude of laborers, were plazas of varying sizes and two game fields equidistant from one another within the wooden walls. Groups of lesser houses and lush gardens subdivided Cahokia.

Artisans, along with politicians and priests, primarily lived within these massive walls. Their skills included pottery creation, basket weaving, tool crafting, fiber, jewelry and metal making, the etching and ornamentation of shells and pearls and hide and leather preparation. Long ago, he had been one of these designers and had developed and fashioned agricultural implements and weapons for hunting and warfare.

Much occurred outside of the walls of the mighty city. And this area complimented the city and was considered the city as well.

Kakeokoke had walked the city from its borders to its center.

The industries of salt making and primitive copper mines and its associated production flourished here.

Farming settlements, with lesser fortification than Cahokia's core, sprinkled the region that lived upon the bounty of the rivers flowing here. In these scattered settlements and the fields in between, crops beyond corn, beans and squash were made abundant. Pumpkins, tobacco and sunflowers were tilled with the flint and bone hoes that they pieced together in abundance in the city center.

Hunters used the finely honed bow and arrow, snares and traps to kill bison, deer, wild turkey, geese and ducks. Kakeokoke had brought down a bison singlehandedly.

Dugouts and canoes, packed with the finest of furs, produce and other trade objects plied toward and away from Cahokia. The success of their trade was manifest in so much of the abundance that saturated this city. Kakeokoke patted his own belly and grinned. The grin was so unlike a priest but he didn't care for the sheer pleasure of his proud reflections about his people and his city.

Right at his feet, within the walls, ran a creek that was a paradise for young men to learn how to fish. So much was caught in this river miniature. If he had a spear presently, he was most assuredly capable of bringing up catfish, sunfish or bass from the burbling ribbon of water.

But crops were proving difficult of late.

That's why this upcoming ceremony must satisfy Katcheena Mondawmin!

CHAPTER 10

SACRIFICING LIFE
FOR LIFE

Katcheena Mondawmin, Goddess of the Corn, was a stern mother of the earth and expected much from her children, the natives of Cahokia. These people, children of their Goddess mother, toiled long and hard for Katcheena Mondawmin's approval which would show itself in a successful and thriving crop.

Kakeokoke had deemed from the reckoning of the Sun calendar that this would be the eve of sacrifice and ceremony. His own heart beat quickened in his desire to please the Goddess mother.

Arrowhead makers had fashioned the jagged edged tools that would pierce the skin of the maiden and let the blood ooze and flow and drip onto the ground; offering one life for the saving of many lives. The arrowheads used in the sacrificial slaying were made of chert, a flint like material, with razor sharp edges to assure the bloodletting. The final arrowhead that would pierce the maiden's heart was of the whitest bone, inscribed with the scroll of the serpent of fertility. Long in point, edges sharper than any fang, this would enter the maiden's beating core and release her spirit to Katcheena Mondawmin.

The maiden herself, never to have known the seed of a man, had seen twenty one slow circuits of the earth around the golden sun. She was of the ripe age to marry and be a mother herself; her own monthly bloodletting, never controlled by men, had come to pass for six seasons now. She was chosen as this eve was to be her own most fertile purpose ever.

She had been given a new name, Keokumana Catori. She was now the maiden of the Snake Spirit of Life and was admittedly frightened, yet honored, at being the chosen one to give up her own life. She knew that she had to perform in this manner for the sake of success within her family and her larger family, her people.

She remained in silence in a spirit filled dwelling, where she was prepared and cared for by other maidens.

Keokumana Catori never uttered a sound as she was washed clean from her shiny pitch black hair to the soles of her feet. Honey mixed with oil of maize and buffalo cream was applied to her skin to make it soft and easily penetrated by the arrows that would send her to the spirit world. She was dressed in a simple fringed sheath made of the softest tanned hide; scraped to create leather, more buttery and pliable than any cloth. Her hair was combed and one thin braid on the right side of her head was coiled into the S shape of the serpent of fertility. A small shell, iridescent with pink and gold and turquoise colors of the sky, was carved into a comb and held this braid in place. It was her single adornment.

This glowing woman sat crossed legged in continued silence in the dimly lit corner of the dwelling. Her eyes were closed as she pondered her honored surrender to the Earth Mother. The other young maidens kept watch over her; gathered together in their own silence and observed their sister from the more brightly lit far side of the dwelling.

A young Cahokia male who had just completed his coming of age ritual was selected to aim the bow and shoot the arrows that would take Keokumana Catori's life and cause her blood to spill in a slow death. While an honor for him, he would remain disguised with the fertility mask of the Serpent. His victim would never see the face of the one who would fashion her demise.

Kakeokoke, Eagle Priest, raised his hands in prayer and began the chanting that would let the people of Cahokia know that the time of sacrifice had arrived. As he continued the loud chanting, the drums began to beat rhythmically and the people of Cahokia chanted as well. Kakeokoke lowered his own hands after indicating to the people to continue their prayers.

The maidens who had cleansed Keokumana Catori stood and gathered around the one who was to appease the goddess with her precious blood. Each of the maidens touched her with the Eagle's feather of blessing and left the dwelling. She stood calmly and followed them out of this house. Escorted by two men, one's face covered by the mask of the predatory Falcon and the other by the mask of the great Eagle; this maiden took her final steps to the top of the highest mound.

At the top of the mound, there was a rack. Keokumana Catori was led there in slow, firm steps. She spread her arms and then her feet so that her limbs formed an X shape. The men tied the leather thongs that were attached to the rack tightly to her wrists and ankles. She became captive and was incapable of movement.

The arrows must meet their marks to appease Katcheena Mondawmin. They must!

The drums and chanting continued until Kakeokoke raised his hands once again. The crowd halted and hushed absolutely. Holding the prayer stick high he cried out, "Buk tu sana, sana obiati, sana sessa!!

"Take this life! It shall be a life for our life now!"

Keokumana Catori cried aloud her last words, "Nuku mi sana Katcheena Mondawmin. Obiati sana, sana sessa!

"I give my life to you, Katcheena Mondawmin. A life for life now!"

The Serpent masked marksman raised his bow, drew back the first arrow of chert, and let it fly through the air, whistling as it pierced Keokumana Catori's right clavicle. She drew back as the arrow parted her flesh, the first blood beginning to spill. She uttered not a sound. She stared directly ahead at the bow that would send the next arrow to pin her. Whoosh! The next arrow sailed through the torch lit area and met her in the left clavicle. Her head fell as she experienced the ripping pain; more blood oozing and dripping from her upper body.

Two more arrows in succession landed in her lower body away from major organs. This was intentionally done to torture the young maiden as the earth is tortured when she is plowed and furrowed and ripped open, to make her ready to receive the seed of the corn.

The arrows penetrated her flesh high on her thighs. She gasped and shut her eyes tightly for a moment. She regained her strength and bravery as she raised her head to dazedly peer at the bow master once again.

This maiden continued the labor of her death in profound and dignified silence.

The final arrow would be welcomed by Keokumana Catori, who, in her mind, screamed, "Take my life now!"

The pure white bone, jagged edged arrowhead flew rapidly through the air and the crowd shuddered when it reached its final destination, her decelerating heart. Red blood, dripping rhythmically, was spurting out of her chest and falling upon the earth, as the light of life went out in Keokumana Catori's eyes. As her spirit left her, the spurting of her blood slowed and drained her life from her.

The final sacrificial motion was taken when Kakeokoke, Eagle Priest, slashed open Keokumana Catori's chest walls and ripped her heart from her; watering the ground with her crimson current, the juice that had once kept her alive.

This fertility ceremony would continue through the night for the people of Cahokia.

Two young males studying to be Shaman would receive the honor of removing Keokumana Catori's body from the rack. They would gently remove the arrows that rendered her lifeless. Her parents stood by, weeping but proud, to receive their daughter's body. They were also given the arrows that had provided the young maiden with the opportunity to save all of their lives. The women, who had readied Keokumana Catori for her sacrifice, now prepared her body for its final resting place in the mound that contained the bodies of other ritually slain females.

Washed once again, Keokumana Catori's body was covered in a bleached lightweight leather shroud and laid within a hollowed out log. She was immediately carried to the burial mound. Her parents blessed her now with the Eagle feather, and the young males placed body, shroud and container within the mound.

The maidens chanted prayers of thankfulness for Keokumana Catori.

The sacrifice was complete.

Only time were to tell if Katcheena Mondawmin had been pleased.

CHAPTER 11

SNAKE SPIRIT

Keokumana Catori, maiden of Snake Spirit of Life gave her being in a brutal sacrifice; her one life for the good of the many lives in Cahokia. Her body just prepared was then carried to its resting place inside the mound. She slumbered eternally now while the rituals of fertility continued on the earth above her. So many other maidens had and would suffer the identical fate to please Katcheena Mondawmin.

The Cahokia, who lived on the edge of the Great River, worshipped this Serpent, the Snake Spirit of Life. The interlocking scrolled 'S' represented that Serpent as snakes curled in motifs on tattoos, hairstyles and an adornment for the Cahokia individual's body. The symbol was carved into wood, animal bones, plants and shells. This god, and a multiplicity of other gods, was deeply revered by the citizens of the city.

During the continuation of the fertility rites, the Snake Serpent of Life was a visible sign on every person present. The symbol of the black serpent honored the life giving force it represented. Even the smallest baby wore the sign of the Snake in the wrapping leather of the papoose.

Drum beats rhythmically called the Cahokia to stay and share in the fertility ceremony. Couples who had been chosen that evening by Kakeokoke, Eagle Priest, in a lifelong matrimonial bond, made their way to the front of the crowd. They would be blessed to go forth and be successful in creating life within the new union.

Small dwellings, dimly lit, had been prepared by the maidens for the couples. The newly blessed couples would spend the night, cementing their individual relationships in the lovemaking that would join them together as one.

Drum beats changed to call the Cahokia closer. Chanting men announced that the Snake Spirit of Life was near. Women danced and sang sharp trills to beg the Snake Spirit to share the gift of life.

Mikilenia, anxious to experience this rite, looked for his fascination, Anteekwa, and saw her countenance among the maidens. He moved closer to her and once again communicated from his mind into hers. She peered upward to see him and blushed. Once composed, she nodded her head as he approached with a finger to his lips. He reached his hand to hers and she grasped his palm gently but firmly with eyes alive.

Kakeokoke raised his hands to still the drum beats, the chanting and the singing.

All was quiet as the fertility ceremony began.

One couple, Chuabuk and his woman, Kinekana, who had been blessed in the matrimonial bond, represented all within the rite that would begin now.

With Kakeokoke's drawing stick, Kinekana formed two lines in the dirt that were separate yet rounded and appeared to look like the outer nether lips of a woman. Within those lines, two smaller curved lines were also drawn. A finely polished round red garnet was placed at the top of the inner lines. This represented the jewel of the woman. At the bottom of the inner lines, a hole was poked with the drawing stick. Meal from maize, ground from the seeds of the last successful crop, was sprinkled around this indentation in the earth.

Anteekwa watched as Kinekana drew on the earth. Mikilenia was stirring her once again within her mind. Her body was beginning to warm with the interpretation of what she was feeling. When the red jewel was placed, Mikilenia once again inserted his long fingers into

Anteekwa's moist fount, and gently pinched her jewel between his invisible fingers. She began to swoon as she watched what would happen next.

Chuabuk took over his part of the rite at this time. Kakeokoke presented Chuabuk with the prayer stick. Chuabuk held the prayer stick and waved it over the writhing and coiled black snakes contained in a large and tightly woven basket nearby. The presence of the Snake Spirit of Life was here.

Chuabuk raised the prayer stick, which now would represent the male, and began a slow movement to penetrate the hole sprinkled with the meal, the ground seeds of life. Lifting the prayer stick again and again, Chuabuk penetrated the hole, deeper and deeper, deeper and deeper. He held the prayer stick steady and beads of sweat glistened on his brow even in the night.

Seemingly miraculous now, a liquid began forming where the prayer stick entered the opening in the ground. The liquid from the milk wood stick oozed a creamy liquid that filled up the opening. Exhausted, yet excited at the success of the prayer stick in his hands, Chuabuk slowly stopped his thrusting motions.

Mikilenia's own breath quickened, as he felt penetration with Anteekwa. No more dreams, no more pretending. He must have her physically and soon. His bulging loin cloth barely covered his growing member and he had no desire to hide that.

Kakeokoke pronounced the fertility ceremony successful and proclaimed that the Snake Spirit of Life and the superior god, Katcheena Mondawmin, would surely be pleased. Wahkakiya watched over them all.

The newly blessed couples embraced when Kakeokoke opened his arms toward them. One couple at a time, they took their leave to enter the dwellings to consummate their matrimony, and to hopefully create the seeds of new beginnings this night.

Mikilenia embraced Anteekwa briefly. He followed with a hard kiss that was urgent with need. He took her by the hand and began to lead her to one of the dwellings prepared for the blessed couples. He had seen that not all the dwellings were occupied.

As they approached the little hut with the thatched roof, Mikilenia lifted Anteekwa into his arms and carried her quickly inside.

Everything that they would need for their joining was ready for them.   ·

CHAPTER 12

TISWIN'S MAGIC

Inside this small dwelling they found a rough oak table and on that table was a simple meal that had been provided to give them energy for this night. All the huts had been so garnished with food. There were dried buffalo meat, flat bread cooked over the fire, dried peaches collected from the harvest last autumn, and tiswin, the magic ale of the corn.

She drank of the tiswin only. He did not partake of anything at all.

A bed on the floor, lined with down feathers of ducks from the river and covered with the buttery soft leather, called to them.

Mikilenia carried Anteekwa to this thick cushion on the floor. He placed her gently on the leather and knelt beside her. He took her face into his hands and began to kiss her rose stained lips ever so gently. The kissing continued and his serpent-like tongue darted between Anteekwa's lips to seek the inside of her mouth.

Anteekwa's amber eyes flickered with the lamp light fire. She began to untie her braids, removing the small blue feathers first. When her braids were undone, Mikilenia began to comb his fingers through her hair. Her scalp tingled and she raised her chin and proffered her neck to him. He could not resist sampling her there. He even lanced her delicate skin enough to give rise to several drops of blood.

This spurred both of them on! His lust became a furnace and hers an infinite tunnel of ember ready to flame.

She raked her hands through his hair and held him to her neck. She moaned and softly panted as he continued to suckle on her throat and pulled her hair firmly as he did this.

Anteekwa began to fall backwards onto the bed, but Mikilenia held her up. He wanted to ravish her more, but needed to remove the tunic she wore.

"Lift your arms lovely woman."

And with this utterance of his, Anteekwa's arms seemed to rise of their own accord as Mikilenia stirred to lift the material from her. She was beautifully exposed to him; lushly open and he saw her absolute reality, as he had seen her with his seer's power and vision earlier.

He was sexually speared by the string of pearls interspersed with tiny shiny bored beads made from mussel shells that she wore around her taut and narrow waist. He had never been witness to ornamentation of this kind in this location before. His cock expanded immensely as he stared momentarily.

He moved to assist her to a supine position. Mikilenia wanted to drink in her form before he took her as his own. Her pendulous breasts spread out to the sides and mounded deliciously too as her flesh was so ample there. Her nipples were the deepest black that he could imagine! There were virtually no aureoles and her thick nipples were in the exact center of her mildly heaving tanned globes; the aureoles unnecessary. He was unable to look away from her. His lips, tongue and teeth followed his greedy eyes.

He moaned when her nipples puckered inside his mouth. Like the deep colored kernels of dried maize, they became very firm with his ministrations to them. He let them roll around his tongue as he suckled her. Her moans surpassed his own.

Anteekwa's back arched as she pulled his hair once again. She wanted him to have her soon!

They rolled off the cushion onto the hides littering the remainder of the hut's surface. Inadvertently, she pushed the thatched opening ajar and their movements and sounds became visible to the gaping celebrants.

He was lying atop her and she reached down and pulled his loin cloth to the side. She wanted to touch his thick shaft, his prayer stick that would give her pleasure and fulfillment. His cock was massive and hardened like the wood of that prayer stick. The tip flared out like the biggest of the arrowheads. No jagged edges though; all was smooth and supple on the surface, so steely on the inside.

She was certain that once he entered her that there would be no stopping them prior to release.

He stroked between her legs and found her flooded center. She was hot and sticky and slick for him. He took some of that wetness from her and massaged her jewel until it felt polished under his fingertips. She trembled and circled her hips subtly as he did this to her.

Mikilenia then brought his fingers up to her lips and gently inserted his finger into her mouth. She tasted herself on him and desperately wanted more of him!

Mikilenia kissed her passionately and powerfully once again.

He moved himself between her legs, raising her knees with his hands. She opened wide for him, brought her knees up to her chest and felt his dew drop that had formed, dripping now against her opening.

Anteekwa wanted to feel him inside her and sought him out by wrapping her legs around his back and bringing him toward her with her heels.

Her eyes spoke the word before her lips could form it, "Please! Oh, please!"

Mikilenia was gentle no longer. He had to have her this instant! He set his aching cockhead against the suffused flesh of her opening. Their aches multiplied immeasurably at this contact. He then plunged his staff into her hard. His cock reached the deep ring of muscle that was inside of her. It excited him no end and he thrust potently and rapidly into her.

With every thrust, Anteekwa cried out, "Unh! Unh! Unh!" over and over!

They came so close to releasing quickly. He did not want to climax abruptly, so he slowed almost to a stop.

"Wait! We will wait!" he uttered between gasps.

"No! Keep going! Do it! Do it!" She let her nails bite into his buttocks in her desire.

He succumbed to her pleas and the swift pounding of his cock into her opening made Mikilenia give up his prior restraint. He had one end in mind for the both of them. He wanted this time, their first coupling, to be the most intense. In his mind, he coached her on.

"Now beauty, reach the stars and sun and moon with me! Come to the edge of light joined!"

Anteekwa held tightly to him, bucking her hips to meet him and found her heat. The heat spread out over her and washed her in the exquisite pleasure that Mikilenia found at the same time. He grunted and groaned as his milk of life and pleasure filled her up. She moaned and cried out and the stars burst inside her.

Her muscles clenched him like the jaws of an underworld deity and he spasmed like a thundercloud inside her.

The Snake Spirit of Life appeared in the doorway briefly. Transparent and silent, the deity nodded in approval.

The couple never took notice.

The crowd most assuredly had taken notice of all.

CHAPTER 13

DECIDEDLY REPULSED

They had been situated above the celebrants on a hardly elevated, flattened mound upon the temple mound where the sacrifice had just been performed. Great Eagle, Kakeobuk, and his small entourage of Minkitooni, Mahkwa and Ashkipaki sat astride what was the equivalent of a royal booth. The view was magnificent and even with the inefficient light of torches placed erratically, not a nuance of activity was missed by these four. And of course, as the undead, that was to be expected.

Minkitooni understood the huge irony, the grand paradox, of a vampire being decidedly repulsed by her first time spectacle of the savage rites performed at her feet. And to also have witnessed the profound writhing, chanting and dancing humans as these events occurred was more revolting.

Humans were despicable; not most vampires. Even when feeding, in her estimation, life was taken quickly by a vampire with a regard for the misery of the victim. What she observed here was blatant torture and then cherished copulation after. Mikilenia and the Cahokia woman, a princess no less, had the temerity to expose themselves while wildly engaged.

She paused. Obviously not all vampires were so careful of their prey nor were decent in the diminishment of pain and cruelty;

Mikilenia was deemed a sorry creature by Minkitooni. How had she ever sought his arms or bore his children?

Minkitooni looked askance at her love, Kakeobuk. She then gauged his and the two others reaction via her seer capacity and they did the same with her simultaneously. The group was shocked to some degree. She, though, was, by far, affected the most.

She would persuade them all now! She had to convince them that this barbarous behavior had to be banished quickly. There was no other recourse. Her pure heart, though undead, was not capable of tolerating the mass flow of blood, cruelly inflicted pain for the satisfaction of wretched and invisible gods.

Kakeobuk was immediately and sharply aware of Minkitooni's repulsion of the sacrifice and what she obviously thought of as inappropriate antics after the fact of the virgin death. What caught him momentarily off guard though was his recognition of Ashkipaki's negative sentiments to be nearly equal those of Minkitooni's and her fervent recoil from the events that had just played out before them.

Mahkwa was neutral as was Kakeobuk.

The fierceness of Ashkipaki's revulsion obviously revolved around her son's delight in the rivers of red blood exposed in the ritual and his crass and oblivious engaging of intimate behavior with a woman who was virtually unknown to him. That Ashkipaki, once having engaged sexually with this son of hers, was reacting in such a conventional manner was a total and complete jolt to Kakeobuk. And she was a vampire as well. Rivers of blood and lusty fornication were staples to their kind!

But Kakeobuk was learning gradually that even his kind were not immune to finding offense in behaviors that contained a razor's edge. He felt it within himself, for sure. He, through Minkitooni and Ashkipakis' eyes, saw the reprehensible facets of being guided only by primal and reptilian instincts. His definite love for Minkitooni and her pristine heart had softened the vile edges of his rapid desires.

And Ashkipaki's heaving bosom and rasping and harsh breath beside him set him to finding fault with the deaths of the innocent.

As Minkitooni turned her head his way, Kakeobuk took her hand and nodded in affirmation. Mahkwa did the same with Ashkipaki. There was no anticipation of satisfying sexual cravings here and now. Tenderness and understanding was to be sought after and laid out in the softest of gestures and words.

The men swirled with the sense that they were to hold their opinions and judgments in reserve in order to capture and preserve the more vocal and righteous sentiments of the female beating hearts alongside them.

Mahkwa spoke first. "Cherished leader, you must give signal for the celebration to cease and desist now."

Ashkipaki hissed out her agreement as Minkitooni curbed her reactions barely! "My son learned nothing those many years ago with me! He still knows nothing of restraint and the bounds of some kind of civility. I almost disown him at this very moment. Blood does not give up on blood though and I will stand in front of him soonest and speak my truth to him. This is a disgraceful thing!"

Minkitooni was shocked at Mikilenia's carryings on with this mortal woman but was more alarmed and livid at the fact of the innocent maiden's slaying; and so roughly with much torture involved. Her legs trembled at the images that beset her presently.

"This has to stop at once Kakeobuk! All of it! There is no sanction in my mind for the cruelty occurring in the slaughter of that brave maiden in her torture and death for gods that do not even exist!

"If you do not command them to end these celebrations, my love, I will wail for them to do exactly that!"

Kakeobuk simultaneously put a restraining hand upon her arm to impede her from doing anything outrageous and with his other arm waved it at Kakeokoke to halt all activity on this night.

It would be done regardless of his brother's understanding. It would be done immediately or The Great Eagle would stride to the center of all and end it himself. And that would begin with the death of his brother.

Kakeokoke needed no goading from his beloved sibling and shouted out a chant that caused all activity to conclude and the crowds to disperse.

CHAPTER 14

FURTHER RIFT

All the vampires and Kakeokoke and Anteekwa retreated to the mound that was the true home of the undead in Cahokia.

It was there that the rift that had already been born earlier became huge and further alienated Mikilenia and Anteekwa from the others.

The others were certain that maiden sacrifice and the antics after were to be curtailed instantly.

Mikilenia and Anteekwa were aghast; Mikilenia in order to appease his singularly wild appetites and Anteekwa in order to preserve what was a tribal ritual that had occurred before and throughout her life.

With Mikilenia by her side, Anteekwa was heady and bold in expressing forthrightly her outlook upon the issue. As if it was a prideful thing, she spoke these words, "Have any of you who are newly begotten in this land of mine ever seen the largest of the tombs for our dead?"

Minkitooni replied, "You will not impress me no matter what you say or describe to me!"

"Your mind is frayed presently and you will see the reason behind my words."

Mikilenia held his tongue for once as he discerned that Anteekwa, as a member of the elite of the city, one who was not of the undead and was not a slave to his brother's wishes, was persuasively in her element.

"Power resides in our burial mounds.

"There is the power, as you are well aware my Great Uncles, in offering repose to our revered leaders. Did we all not participate in the burial of the Great Falcon who led before you oh Great Eagle? Did we not lie him down upon a multitude of our loveliest shell beads to make a beautiful bed for his eternal sleep? Did we not shape the beads into the superb design of the falcon with its head underneath his human head? And were we not careful to position the wings and tail of the magical bird below his arms and legs so that he could fly to the spirit world? And we gave him arrowheads of the best design and craftsmanship to allow him to fight all demons that might attempt to waylay him upon his journey?"

"This means nothing to me, Princess!" Minkitooni nearly screamed this in Anteekwa's face.

Ashkipaki spat out, "We wish to stop the foolish sacrifices, not prevent burials!"

The brothers and Mahkwa were steely faced and glowered at Anteekwa and Mikilenia.

Mikilenia glowered back and placed his large arm around his new found love's waist. He evinced no retreat and silently encouraged Anteekwa to say more!

"You have no understanding of the necessity that sacrifice and then disposal of those bodies means to the crops, the safe passage of our spirits to the invisible land of our ancestors and continued fertility of our kind . . . of which many of you are not!"

Kakeobuk commanded silence suddenly. And it was the entity inside him that uttered harshly to Anteekwa and Mikilenia a charged response that brooked no disagreement!

"Silence! All!

"The cherished females who stand at the sides of Kakeokoke, Mahkwa and I remind us of the nature of the cruelty that occurs in each and every woman lost to the might of our ritual arrows. They pierce her skin and her blood and life slowly ooze from her.

"We lose some of the best of our citizens in this manner! And yes, they submit and give heroically to the interests of our tribe, our city and our continued survival. But they, as do you Anteekwa, believe in gods, primitive gods that do not exist!"

Kakeobuk pointed his long and narrow finger at Mikilenia and splashed these words onto the rebelling vampire's face, "You know that as we undead all know that!

"I am the ancient vampire and have lived as such longer than anyone in this cavernous room. I am Cain and Lilith's son.

"I see the corpses that have been casually piled in heaps in the vast mound that you speak of, Anteekwa. There is no respect or dignity in the discarding of the remains of the slaughtered to the gods. There are corpses rotting, hands and feet missing, countless virgin maidens tossed together with no regard for their spirits. Some reach up with their hands and arms as if still alive and still attempting to struggle up and out of the mass of bodies.

"And for what?!

"That they feed the endless needs of the gods above?

"I know! There are no gods. These gods do not exist. I have lived for what feels an eternity. And there is only a single force superior to me. And what it is, I do not know for certain. Just that I move at the command of this ethereal energy. I am its instrument!

"And it is none of the gods that you or your tribe, my tribe as well, defend and pray to!

"This loss of life is mindless and serves no fundamental purpose!

"And this joining of men and women in the flesh after the sacrifice shall not continue either as it is simply a taunt to the being beyond me!"

Minkitooni, Ashkipaki, Mahkwa, Kakeokoke all intoned their respective agreement.

Minkitooni was fully fused to her love now in the wisdom that he had made word.

Mikilenia spat blood in Kakeobuk's direction, lifted Anteekwa, spun on his heel and burst from the chamber.

Kakeobuk raged internally that this unruly vampire whose skin had once been his would burn with his wrath if he did not obey soon!

CHAPTER 15

VAMPIRE'S ITCH

He scratched at his damnable ankle itch, a tiny patch of red there that he had carried for a long while, and then refocused attention on his lovely paramour, Ashkipaki. They lounged alone in their chamber presently.

"My love, you don't recall your son being this rash and determined to have his way in all of our wanderings after he joined us, do you?"

He unconsciously slapped at a tiny black object that hopped and was gone.

"It was hundreds of years that we dallied in the continent where Cinaed brought together the broken pieces of that smaller land; the land that they called Scotland.

"What do you remember first of that period of ours, Mahkwa?"

"I recall the ragged energy of the hoard of followers of the man that many called Peter the Hermit. Our Cinaed then, rebellious Mikilenia now, lusted after the female zealots who pursued Peter to their eventual slaughter. These women were infused with a radiant energy that Cinaed seemed unable to resist. And he pursued their blood only after they succumbed to his sexual feasting upon them. He was rampant and they delighted in being his sacrificial lambs.

"Even when the mob, seeking the Holy Land, reached only the domain of the Turks where they were sadly and haplessly slaughtered, even then, the free and copious flow of red and rich sustenance did not engage Cinaed as he is engaged now! I saw no evidence of any behavior as outrageous as he performs here in the mounded city."

"He flexed his impulses then, I fully agree. But he never found a total disregard for alliances or boundaries as he does with Kakeobuk." Ashkipaki was quietly stunned as she and Mahkwa reviewed the trio's behavior prior to arriving in Cahokia.

"What then?" she continued.

"We all relished the reign of King John Lackland as Cinaed became his enforcer. When Cinaed killed and then took over the identity of William De Wendenal, Sheriff of Nottingham, he became John's most able ally. He cherished applying the rules of his harsh master. And Cinaed was often harsher than his master in levying taxes, keeping the commoner from poaching on King's lands and dispatching brigands who opposed the King.

"But there was never a moment, even when John was forced to sign that horrible document and Cinaed looked on in anguish and anger that evening, where he lost his mind as he seems to have lost it now.

I fear for the clash between Kakeobuk and Mikilenia if it comes to that! Mikilenia would be an utter fool to think that he could overcome the primacy and power of the entity, Kakeobuk!"

Ashkipaki trembled for her son. "Mikilenia was magnificent when the floods sought the terrain of Europe. We were magnificent in equal measure to him.

Water poured into most of our earthen sanctuaries. Our motivation may have been a bit of desperate selfishness as our chambers of repose were being destroyed but we all found our determination to build banks of mud and stone together to defend against the greater damage that was being wrought by the steady rains that we experienced then."

"The wetness seeped through everything it seemed. Cinaed toiled with the rest of us to salvage what we could of land and damp spaces." Mahkwa shuddered at the thought of water penetrating all soils, cracks and crevices.

He continued. "Then there was that onslaught of death that we all observed. If we had not been of infinitely permanent flesh, we too would have fallen prey to what was seeking out the lives of so many others.

"It was a horrible thing to encounter, even for our kind: our kind ever familiar with an abundance of spilt blood and limp flesh.

"Our seer abilities were clear, too clear often, in informing you, me and Cinaed of what the victims suffered. Oh my god, to be witness to that was crushing as we had to drink the blood of the already ravaged dying and the mercilessly gutted dead.

"I almost felt the very sensations that the victims of this disease were crippled by. My head pounded viciously until I controlled the strength of the image in my mind. I did this with each and every stage of the black scourge. Chills and furious fever laid most in its path low and exhausted. Then there came the nausea, vomiting, back pain and then pain everywhere.

"The worst followed. Lumps, hard lumps, formed on the neck or armpits or the inner thighs. Those small fists of flesh turned a raven color then, swelled, cracked in half and then ushered out pus and blood.

I am vampire. And I nearly was brought to my knees with a gorge almost pouring forth from my throat!"

"And the atrocious smell of the alive but rotting bodies, wasting from their insides out, was almost beyond even our comprehension!" Ashkipaki hugged herself to stop her quivering as she recollected the oh so grisly scene and spectacle of death all around; mean death, impossibly hideous death.

That which was of such a groaning and grievous impact upon the undead was staggering indeed!

"Cinaed held up well throughout a continent cupped with corpses." Mahkwa had been impressed at the stalwart nature that the one who was now Mikilenia showed then.

"What then," Ashkipaki asked, "was the last event that might have tested Cinaed's resolve to be rational?"

"He had opportunity to deny Jack Straw life and take that man's identity to his bosom but did not as he felt no desire then to be unruly. He seemed tired of finding nourishment in the guise of men who chose to shake the very foundations of society.

Then he awoke to her location and we flanked his flight and found ourselves in the grasslands between rivers here."

That was the wound that Mikilenia was presently suffering! His mother knew it suddenly and told Mahkwa.

"His loss of Minkitooni drives him berserk. And we can do nothing to stop the harm that will descend!"

CHAPTER 16

ITCH RELIEVED

Even through her various prominent blue tattoos, she was shockingly pale. And she was unable to contain her building shivers even as she clasped her knees and rocked. It was incessant and escalating; the chambers warmth did not help whatsoever.

Their vile but urgent and obligatory reminiscences had brought this on. Ordinarily, Ashkipaki and Mahkwa avoided study of those tumultuous years of the three of them together. It had been challenge enough to have managed their connection for one another in spite of the mayhem and ugliness of those times. To recollect them added to the abuse and was only performed in acute necessity . . . as was now!

Kakeobuk, his brother and Minkitooni had fled the area hours ago to seek out and calm Anteekwa and Mikilenia. So the two remaining vampires had had time to sort amongst the facts and arrive at an adequate explanation for her son's volatile recent behavior. It was excessive and might prove deadly as well. If the vampires fought, likely the demise of one or more would occur.

Mahkwa went to Ashkipaki immediately. As he scooted in next to her, he hugged her about her shoulders and then he softly rubbed his hands over the discontent of the skin of her arms. He also murmured in her ear. He whispered this to her, "You are correct. But we will find a way to soothe all." "Soothe all," he repeated again and again; the words carried upon his warm and tender breath to her soul's embrace.

She was soothed as he caressed her so lovingly.

He cherished this love of his; this tender, even if undead, woman, this Ashkipaki. They plied much history together and he had turned her. Then when he fell out due to the entity's exit, she had turned him again.

And she responded to his gentle but equally overwhelming concern and strong waves of support and love for her. And that response went to her fundaments, her fountain of joy. And that fountain glistened and flowed for him.

As she relaxed into his huge arms and massive hands, he tenderly kissed her neck until she shivered again. But these shivers were now of sparking passion, not of awful fear. She straightened and turned her face towards him. As she did this, he had had to stop his kissing of her neck to pull his head away minutely in order to see the sheen of her eyes, the desire for him there.

He rose to his knees and placed lips of his upon lips of hers. It was divine. Her lips were full, ripe and begging for further of his indulgences. He did just that; he indulged her. And then he indulged himself.

They were lavish and lascivious with one another; and were unable to contain the flame from this point on.

He was delighted anew each and every time that he inhaled her Cahokia look. She had multiple feathers in her long dark and now braided hair. There was a gleam to the raven tones that the blue, the yellow, the bright crimson feathers brought out. The contrast was superb. And the long braids gave her a young appearance in addition. His cock flared as he thought these delicious thoughts.

And then there were the shiny mussel shells that had the tiniest of bored holes so as to hang from necklaces and even a special waistband that she alone had fashioned. They begged for touch and the style of beads around a woman's waist and hips was fast becoming overwhelmingly popular amongst the women of the city. And they made him lust for her nonstop.

He felt her necklace and then let his hands drift down to her chest. Her tunic was buttoned with the same mussel shell pieces and he released them instantly. He was not able to wait any longer. Her very heavy breasts poured forward and bobbled wondrously. She was of lean, tiny stature and short torso so that her mounds filled up most of her upper body. He stroked her there in automatic rapture.

She arched her chest out to his hands whereupon he cupped her curves momentarily and then pinched and twisted her also very large, very hard black points of flesh at the perfect centers of each of her breasts.

He was feeling urgency for her and so he shifted his position in order to face her frankly and hotly. He no longer chose to be positioned beside her. And as soon as he fronted her he bent to suckle at those nipples that he had been touching with his fingers only moments ago. He went side to side with his mouth and she moaned for his contact without restraint.

While his mouth was upon one finger of turgid dark flesh, he squeezed the other nipple hard. He squeezed and then he pulled. What roused her most at this point was when he would suck her point into his mouth and gently rub the edges of his teeth against the dark flesh and, simultaneously, pull, twist and squeeze her other nipple. She quaked and cried out his name as he did this.

Mahkwa was stretched to his maximum. His cock felt hugely thick and long.

She clutched at his loincloth. It could have been moved aside but she simply ripped it off of his chiseled waist.

His cock was throbbing and felt like a warriors club.

He had his passion dew that she elicited for him when they were like this and it dripped from his opening and slowly oozed to the underside of his cock. She lifted her head and removed his hands from her breasts. She wanted to lead and she would lead. Mahkwa craved her lead as well.

She gazed at his vast manhood and its gushing clear liquid and she experienced the swelling of her crown jewel and its wanton shining ruby redness. Her core poured forth her own flooding wetness. And then she took a thumb and massaged his clear precome all over his plum purplish cockhead. He grew even more under the sensation of that thumb of hers.

His growls enflamed her moans and they were tempest tossed now; riding the thunderous wave that was their own.

She pumped his member hard and fast. He stopped her so that his come was postponed for just a bit.

He lay upon his back as he understood her always greatest desire with him. He peered up at her with dumbstruck and ardent eyes and spread his legs wide. The slight involuntary motion of his occasionally jerking cock filled midair and she approached it with lathered desire.

She backed onto his cock as he guided it in to her. The fit was incredible as always. They both gasped at the fitting of cock and holster.

She began to pound onto him as he etched pale indentations into her ass as he gripped her there. He spread her buttocks as she was heaving against him.

She felt the vibration throughout her clit and then to her torso and then to her throat and face. It was pushing her to the vortex of her climax. The spread of her ass cheeks was the final goad that released her heaven bound. She sat upright as if shot into that position and ground her hips against his cock and groin. The spasms exploded out of her and kept exploding. Each burst saturated her pleasure centers more than the last. And it seemed never ending.

His cock core underwent a rhythmic squeezing from her ecstatic release and he was helpless then.

Involuntarily his cock unleashed mammoth amounts of pearlescent come into her deepest spaces. He poured so much that, as they were gasping in the aftermath of it all minutes later, come slid from around the edges of where his cock joined her flesh.

Their itch had been relieved in such a manner as to think that they would never again require it.

But of course they would.

CHAPTER 17

NATURE'S FORCE

Kakeobuk's master foresaw this phenomenon but allowed only vampire seer sight to function just enough for survival of those undead. Communication to all others was forbidden.

Moisture surrounding Cahokia massed and lifted upward into the atmosphere.

It was a force of nature, albeit rare, and an occurrence for this region; the reality was not so much the happening, as rain fell regularly here, or had, but it was the vast size of the movement developing swiftly.

A thermal had been provoked from the grounds accumulated heat. Though more cool than was familiar, Cahokia had undergone a spell of rain's absence. The cool temperatures had been wrestled aside temporarily and it had been even more intensely hot and humid than was customary.

This thermal drove the saturated air upwards. The speed of the pack of moisture's rise was extreme. Temperatures surrounding the moisture dropped as the pack itself exploded upward into the sky.

Droplets formed as the warm air and the cool air overlapped and combined.

Cumulus clouds, dark and thick, developed with the potential for near instant crescendo of liquid falling.

Beneath this incipient threatening pillow filled to the bursting with water was a vacuum of low pressure below that had swooped in to replace the originally vacated area. It moved in as viciously as the former had moved out.

This created a vortex that was to suck the dew from the sky and pound over the hapless city of Cahokia.

It was not of Wahkakiya but of forces beyond primitive comprehension that blended in such a precise manner that the outcome was predictable.

The heaving storm, predictable in its onslaught, began now.

Relief was to be slow and stubborn no matter the appeals.

After an indeterminate amount of time, human voices were heard above the din of the rain.

"He-ay-hee! He-ay-hee! Hohahe, Wahkakiya! He-ay-hee! Na ma sota! Na ma sota! Kiksuyapi ina maka!

He-ay-hee! He-ay-hee! Hohahe, Wahkakiya! He-ay-hee! Na ma sota! Na ma sota! Kiksuyapi ina maka!"

The Cahokia populace, drenched to the bone, chanted incessantly from the highest of the mounds.

"We call to the Great Spirit, Wahkakiya, and our Thunderbird. Please halt the many waters! Remember Mother Earth!"

There had been great anger in the sky, and the people would suffer by displeasing Wahkakiya they believed.

What had they done to offend their Eagle God so?

The mighty Wahkakiya created the storm as it flew over Cahokia, determined to enforce its distinct and ferocious antipathy, by causing Mother Earth to endure the blows of the glorious Thunderbird's wrath.

The flapping of the Great Thunderbird's wings caused the clouds to clash together and created the deafening noise that caused even the bravest of Cahokia to recoil in fright.

Lightning flashed from Wahkakiya's eyes, and it dropped the killing liquid in the form of glistening and writhing snakes carried in its massive, razor-sharp talons.

These serpents crashed to the defenseless and dry ground in their glee. The serpents then splashed into an array of exploding droplets and ground their way into Mother Earth's dusty bosom.

There was barely a way of telling how many times the light of day was separated from the darkness of night during the catastrophic storm. The skies were such a seriously intense grey.

There was no letup in the destructive torrential rains that fell upon Cahokia. It appeared that Wahkakiya's fury lasted through three cycles of the sun. But no one was certain of how truly long the heaven's blast had continued.

The parched and suffering soil could no longer absorb the rainfall. Rain that usually brought life to the crops now devastated the community and pounded all life upon the land into submission.

Stalks of maize lay submerged, bent and snapped in the distress of the relentless rainfall and those stalks were now useless as food for immediate consumption or even storage for later use. Mud had oozed over so much that was not already covered in water.

The mighty Wahkakiya ceased flight over Cahokia. This Thunderbird had eventually heard the pleading chants of the people.

The punishment had been carried out.

The sky, still a deep slate grey, threatened overhead. The slashing volley stopped.

The people of Cahokia discontinued their chanting and fell silent.

Wahkakiya had shown little mercy to these people. Once a population of twenty thousand, these urban Indians had gradually been reduced to ten thousand, and now, looking out over the city of Cahokia, it became evident that their population had fallen even more so in the overwhelming system of weather brought on in the last seventy two hours.

Mother Earth had been attacked savagely.

The torrential rain that came upon her in Cahokia increased and covered her in a devastating and destructive blanket of water; only the inner and upper mounds had not been penetrated by the watery ravages. Surely Mother Earth's flesh would decay with the massive injuries she sustained from Wahkakiya's wrath.

CHAPTER 18

AN ILL OMEN

S aturated sod engulfed his feet and Kakeokoke ventured to peer down from the mound, the mound that preserved some life as many had fled here for safety; those who could and had the moment to escape before the sheets of rain swallowed them whole.

His shoulders carried the weight of his people as he motioned for them to stay where they were while he ventured out to determine Wahkakiya's damage.

Kakeokoke began his trek down from the highest mound. The clouds had begun to part and the sun's presence indicated that daylight was at hand.

Trees were torn out by the roots and toppled over like vegetables just harvested from the garden. Mudslides threatened every footstep; and in that one false move might send scores of his brethren into the swollen Mississippi, Missouri and Illinois Rivers below.

The houses, built in such sturdy fashion and lined up side by side, suffered the storm's demolition and appeared like eggshells crushed underfoot from the trampling of a nest and everything had been thoroughly ground up.

Kakeokoke raised his hand to speak to the people.

"I speak for my beloved brother who is so sad at the destruction and devastation experienced by us here in Cahokia that his grief renders him speechless for the moment.

"Wahkakiya has pummeled Cahokia.

"Wahkakiya thinks much of our people or there would be nothing left of Cahokia at all.

"We must search and find our people who have survived.

"Together we are safe. Together we are strong. Together we will overcome. Let us begin the new journey arm in arm immediately."

Activity continued swirling around Kakeokoke as he finished his speech of hope, commiseration and a plea for the mercy of the greater and lesser gods.

Fortunate survivors were traveling by the long white cedar canoe as they transported people and goods to the ends of Cahokia.

Salvaged pottery, food and clothing were jam packed into the canoes as the Cahokia populace moved to higher ground.

The native people moved almost in total silence. After the anger of Wahkakiya upon Mother Earth, no one knew quite how to respond. This spirit's violence was beyond what any of them were accustomed to living through.

The water was so high. It covered the lower land, so that the canoes were easily floated through what had been the streets of Cahokia.

Several canoes were collecting the bodies of the women, children and elders which floated on the water's surface. Would their taken lives be accepted as sacrifice? Only Wahkakiya was to decide this.

Other canoes were rescuing survivors who clung to the toppled trees.

One young mother had been so frightened that she could not remove her hands from the branch that she held tightly to for her survival. Her children, lashed tightly to her side, were quiet as she sang to them.

"I will keep you safe my baby birds. Mother Earth provides a nest for us in her tree. Under my wings, I shield you from harm."

She kept singing this softly to her children, over and over.

One of the men, normally strong and brave and not apt to give in to a woman's cries, became himself a gentle man who understood her fright; so he pried her fingers one by one from the branch she clung to and sang to her.

"The time has come to leave the nest. Mother bird, take leave. Your babies will be safe in a nest that has been prepared in the land that has survived."

Sore afraid, she leaned into him heavily and clasped her hands tightly together as she wrapped her arms about his neck. He lowered her and her babes into the canoe. She and hers were safe now.

They had to hurry on. So many like her clung to trees further down this tempest tossed river. They had to rescue more and more of their people from the ravages of the storm.

His words and his touch were not as gentle as time went by and so many had to be released from their secure perches.

One group of men canoed to the most dangerous northern side of the running waters. The chain of rocks here was treacherous and the waters were rapid and speeding by.

On the shore, where the rocks formed a wall not passable by any canoe, the water had risen. Three of the cities farmers were on the shore, yelling and running back and forth; kneeling, standing and kneeling once again, as if in a state of panic.

Motioning for the canoe to come closer, they began to beg for help.

"Wahkakiya have mercy on us! One of your children has been taken to the Great Sky!

Mother Earth weeps at Heaven's cruelty and we are at your mercy!"

The canoe maneuvered over the water covered rocks and was pulled onto the shore by the three panicked males.

There, on the ground, next to the fallen tree bearing her nest was a mother eagle!

Her wings were outspread, as if in supplication, and her head tilted upward with her mouth open, as if she had spoken during her last breath. Her eyes were open as she went to meet her greater Wahkakiya.

"This is an ill omen.

"The fate of this mother eagle will be the fate to befall all of us. Wahkakiya have mercy on us, Mother Earth's children!"

No one was able to calm this man.

There were three eggs in the nest. Two of them were crushed, with the life inside oozing out. One egg remained intact.

The rescuer, the one who had become gentle with the singing woman, picked up the mother eagle and cradled her in his arms. To be touching an eagle, even one that had no life beating within, was truly an honor.

He then placed the body of the eagle on some leather and took the remaining egg, positioned it on her body and wrapped her wings around it to keep it protected.

The aroused Cahokia male shrieked, "If this egg survives, we too may survive!"

The three men from the shore entered into the canoe and were given the task of guarding the mother eagle's body until they reached the highest mound where they would present her to Kakeokoke.

The sky had returned to its grey and threatening appearance.

Neither Wahkakiya nor Mother Earth was pleased now.

This canoe carried these people and the remains of the mother eagle and her surviving egg back to the mounds. There would be no talking, no singing. All would sit in silence, even the little children.

This day they had survived the storms of Wahkakiya, but now they faced even more grave danger as the death of one mother eagle carried with it presumed dire consequences for all.

Hours passed and the vampires roused from their repose. They had been prepared for the thrashing of the land; they had seen it before it struck but had not had opportunity to warn the surrounding citizenry.

They had had simply enough of an interval to fly as a group of bats, another terrifying sight for those who had been witness to it, to Kakeobuk's residence and temple and throw themselves into the darkest rooms that they were able to find.

They survived the meager presence of natural light during the holocaust just come.

None knew of Mikilenia or Anteekwa's whereabouts. No one was seemingly concerned either as other issues engulfed them.

CHAPTER 19

I HAVE DELIBERATED

The water had receded in the near half month since the catastrophic storm had seized the city of Cahokia.

The Grand Plaza had escaped destruction only due to its significant height above the river bottoms.

Kakeobuk stood upon the elevated ceremonial platform in the Grand Plaza with his trusted allies at his side. Minkitooni, Mahkwa, Ashkipaki and his brother took their place to his left and right. The surviving citizenry gathered round their leader with anxious anticipation stirring the air around them.

All of the survivors had been located, rescued and returned to the remains of their city. The fetid bodies of the dead had yet been piled high inside one burial mound awaiting the ceremony of deliverance of these dead to the world beyond. Their journey had to be sanctified by their priests before the bodies could be dealt with properly. It would be done.

The tragedy was that these cadavers rotted as the tribe toiled in the effort of rebuilding a region that had been leveled to scattered debris of flattened buildings, wasted wild and domesticated animals alike and the remnants of splintered and thoroughly fragmented brush, timber and corn stalks. The mounds remained but the obliteration of all at their margins was bleak and overwhelming.

The terrain was grim and the gathering of bodies, let alone their appropriate disposal, had been stymied by the labors of the shocked survivors to clear the ground and rebuild what had once been an imposing and thriving Indian metropolis.

Kakeobuk flamed with the notion that no more individuals were to be sacrificed ever again while he had breath and motion. He was now not only awash in the principle of preserving human life as opposed to its useless sacrifice to utterly fictitious gods but also saw the awful reduction of populace before him. They had to rebuild and recover and they required every able bodied man and woman for this monumental task that was before them.

He comprehended that it was a task that was achievable in unison and cooperation. Would that happen though? Even with concentration of his powers, he was not able to discern the far flung outcome of this natural disaster and the disaster that Mikilenia and Anteekwa might impose upon the land. He would do all that he could to find success here in the midst of disaster and death though.

"My people, I have gathered you here in twilight marked by the many torches because I can no longer tolerate the sun.

"I make no apologies for that. It is so and I must live with this affliction. You must adapt to it as we now must adapt to a crisis that is hard and harsh.

"Our fathers, mothers, brothers, sisters, children have died in the terrible flood waters of our sacred rivers. Water is life but sometimes it is death as well.

"We are at a moment where we survive or pass; I can feel that deeply and severely.

"So I have deliberated with my love, my counselors, my priests and Kakeokoke! We have deliberated long and in earnest and it has not been easy. Nothing I will say to you here and now has been arrived at without huge concern and heavy heart."

Kakeokoke paced a step closer to Kakeobuk's side as the Great Eagle continued speaking. The unification of the two brothers was made obvious by this maneuver. Kakeobuk silently applauded his brother for doing this.

"We performed sacrifices many moons ago to honor our gods of unity, fertility and success. And, as I see it, the gods failed us! We did not fail them!

"We did all that was asked by the spirits above and were utterly smashed in reply!

"Either we displeased our gods, which I cannot conceive of how we failed them whatsoever, or we are serving the wrong gods.

"I have a sight that is so sensitive now that it cannot tolerate any kind of bright natural light. And I see that we, as a people, have made a mistake. There is but a single God and I must now reveal to you that I am spirit made flesh by this God. He moves through me and I pass the power and essence along to you of what has been made manifest to me.

"There will be no more sacrifices. This God is not meant to cripple our culture by asking for our people to be ruthlessly and cruelly destroyed upon It's alter."

The collective gasp of the crowd was long and loud. Their Great Eagle had just annihilated their views and had commanded them to alter their vision of the world.

To some in the massed crowd, there was reason in what had just been proclaimed. How had they deserved the wrath of their god's displeasure when they had so meticulously fulfilled those gods' wishes? That and the anger at lost loved ones gave coloration to some that Kakeobuk had to be correct.

To some others in that same crowd, their fright at abandoning those gods and bringing more punishment upon themselves served to keep them deeply in the fold of their traditions. And they were affronted as well that those cherished gods who had served them well in the past were so callously being left behind.

This divide was immediate and did not change once the initial impulse struck.

The flood was mighty in its devastation but was simply a link in a chain of events that was to pit leader against priest, father against son, brother against brother, wife against husband and more; much more!

The perils to plague this region had just begun.

CHAPTER 20

FOMENT AND DISSENSION

From the moment of his creation as Mezopx, he had hesitated to kill his own kind. He was uncertain of the source of this restraint but it existed as clearly as he existed. He was inclined to blame his master but he had no true inkling as to why this was.

He so desired to swoop down on Mikilenia and snatch all breath from the bastard undead but would not. He could easily slay Anteekwa at this very moment that Mikilenia and she spoke to a smaller crowd where Kakeobuk and his brethren had just made his pronouncement. But she was simply Mikilenia's follower and her death would be meaningless.

Minkitooni nudged him ferociously and he turned to her and simply kissed her and let his seer images explain his predicament to her. She relented as they peered for a moment at the throng wandering the margins of the event platform in the Grand Plaza. He and she blocked their vision of the rebellious vampire and his female whore! They did not choose to see it. The damage of the duo simply had to be dealt with in the soon by and by.

They went to their chamber to find comfort, one for the other. They were disinclined to listen to or see the dissension and foment that Mikilenia and Anteekwa were provoking in the hearts of those antagonized by the words that had sprung from Kakeobuk's mouth to them this very eve.

Obviously, the pair had weathered the storm and floodwaters in order to come back to preach the old gospel of Wahkakiya and the blood required for the land and the city to thrive. It served Mikilenia's goal of driving a wedge into Kakeobuk's power wherever and whenever he could.

Mikilenia shouted to the hordes collected before him that their leader had driven a long spiked shaft and arrowhead through their Thunderbird, their Mother Earth, the Sun, and the Moon. But most especially, he was appealing to their connection to the Serpent God of Fertility and that god's parent, Katcheena Mondawmin, the rites that were due these gods by dint of the writhing bodies of Indians in their huts performing acts of lust and passion.

It was a sacred obligation to present oneself entwined with one of the opposite sex in order to appease and please that god.

The seed of his desire to persuade all in his path was rising. So was the heat of that very same desire finding a smoldering anchor in Anteekwa's breast as well? Mikilenia suddenly felt that he was more able to convince others if he and she were to demonstrate the energy of the Fertility God in the open and before the eyes of the masses. This would encourage those masses to delve into the very same activities; at least all that would succumb to the fuel of Mikilenia and Anteekwa's fire.

Anteekwa saw the affirmation in his eyes and understood exactly what was necessary for her to do next.

The wood of the Plaza's elevated stage was smooth and level providing comfort to any and all activities about to frantically explode.

She allowed her hips to undulate subtly as she reached her arms skyward. The stretch of her arms pulled the fabric of her doeskin tunic hard against her fulsome breasts. The orbs of her aureoles and poke of her very dark nipples revealed themselves to the audience in her gesture and movement.

The band of shell beads that she had applied upon her wasp waist fell to her moving hips. The rise and fall of these beads was mesmerizing as she very well knew that they would be. Mikilenia was frozen in place, lusting for Anteekwa. The only movement of his was the ever lengthening cock that was not about to remain soft. His member had first lengthened as it fattened and fell in the direction of the wood surface. Then his manhood had reached a point of need where the staff of flesh hardened and moved upward swiftly.

Anteekwa was peering at his growing excitement. She rapidly unbuttoned her shell buttons and her globes fell forward and bobbled even as she cupped them and stilled them at the same time. She closed the small distance between him and her until she was able to grasp his now thick and hard shaft in her encircled palm. She gripped it and stroked it. Her firmness was causing his mushroom capped cockhead to turn the color of a plum. It was purple and the veins at the lateral surfaces of this shaft of his throbbed convulsively and in unison.

With her other hand she sucked on one of her fingers for an instant, drew it down between her molten brown breasts, brought it back up to her straining raven hued tips and stroked one, then the other, with the pads and edges of her thumb.

The movement of those remaining in the dark shadows of the Plaza were swaying in a chant of their own, a combined sound that was hushed yet incredibly distinct in its erotic timber and vibration. Male and female bodies turned toward one another and the heat was palpable.

Mikilenia had gotten on one knee by now and sucked avidly at the overripe nipples that Anteekwa presented to him. The tableau was lush and drenched with the fever of the dance and the desire. The Serpent and the Mother were about to entwine.

The vampire stood and then laid his paramour upon the tender surface of the soft wood. She splayed her arms and her legs wide for all to see. She was no longer a sentient creature but was now mindless in her need to be sated by him.

And, as he ripped off her doeskin skirt, he was moving of a will other than his own. It was automatic, strong but love driven as well. He crushed his mouth to the huge swells that were truly his to possess. He kissed and suckled and thrashed about in her flesh there until his huge stick brought his attention elsewhere.

The dark forms who were privy to the coupling of the powerful twosome were no longer chanting. The sounds emanating from below the platform were irregular and alternated between rasps, moans and the sounds of liquid lovemaking.

Mikilenia gently lifted her tiny buttocks up to his rampant cock. She was alert enough to spread her lips and Venus mound broadly for his entry. She did this with thumb and middle finger. She flicked her ruby red jewel with her forefinger.

He mounted her and glided into her wet funnel as if there had been no friction but the most minute. The paradox was that as the friction seemed less and less between his cock and her flesh the greater his build became. The conscious mind receded from them both and the power of the branded joining became everything.

Neither took any notice of the crowd surrounding them. If the noise of the others enjoining reached their ears, it was only noticed on some sublime and subtle level.

He became engorged beyond his prior capacity for size. His organ became massive and her fount became everything. She surrendered first to the demand of release. Her entire body was split with wave upon wave of surging pleasure. His cock experienced this and drove copious amounts of hot and white come into the walls of her inner depths.

She spasmed repeatedly and her hips lifted in a clench that she was unable to control.

He growled as he ground into her bucking center and was pleasured beyond his belief.

If the earlier departing vampires had taken heed and noticed the effect of this display upon the commoner, the Indians writhing in parallel with Mikilenia and Anteekwa, Kakeobuk might have found a means to release his restraint and kill the rebel then and there.

CHAPTER 21

MANGLED MAIZE

The Great Plaza's elevated platform had been almost overused. It had been seven of the earth's rotations since the outrageous display of sensuality had occurred. All involved had long dispersed since and no visible evidence of the event remained.

Kakeobuk stood in the eerie silence of middle night scanning the terrain far and wide. He rotated his head side to side, over and over. This was a habitual and unnecessary movement. He actually had his eyes closed and sought images from the simple seer power that he owned and honed.

So it did not matter that no torches were lit. It did not matter that the palisade walls had resisted the floods surge and loomed in the way of ordinary line of sight. And it did not matter that the land that he assessed was of such a large distance from the plaza.

Scene after scene of destruction swam in his brain. He pitched his vision high, low, in all directions as far as the oceans east and west, gulf waters south and plains and grass of the north.

No crops were spared. The earth was littered with the washed up blades of their chert and buffalo shoulder hoes with almost all handles snapped from the instruments, stone or bone. That the ground was peppered with fragments of the very tool that was used for the tribe's livelihood was unbearable to the Great Eagle.

He was vampire but had been charged by his lord to shepherd this community to a satisfactory continuation. This was his assumption at least. And if it was an erroneous assumption, it was his inclination anyhow.

His edges had been softening for millennia. His external fangs remained large. His internal ones had become dwarfed.

Aztalan, northerly sister city of Cahokia, lay demolished. Their mounds also served as the only reason for the ongoing life and activity there. They were at the same rebuilding stage as were Kakeobuk and his people.

Their crops and foods, as Cahokia's, had been many. Survival relied on a multitude of sources and resources. And it was as if those sources and resources had been decapitated everywhere that the storm had touched.

Secondary foodstuffs, he knew, included knotweed, beans, little barley, squash, marsh elder, sunflower, may grass and goosefoot. These fields were muddied and the initial growth was irrevocably thwarted. The plant life that remained was yellowed and inedible. They required no further tending.

The newness of the sprouts and stalks had been at such a significant and fragile point when the cataclysm struck. Even with tender, moderate weather, some of these baby shoots would die. Now, all of the shoots had been blasted by wind, soaked by rain and floods and were now laid ripped and twisted; entangled one with the next. The muck and plant fiber often were not able to be distinguished.

The wild plants that his people, also the people in the neighboring and outlying areas as Aztalan was, depended upon were churned into leafy masses by Mother Nature's brutality and they were then left soaked beyond recognition by the receding waters.

Wild bean, lotus, arrowhead, grapes, persimmon, sumac, hickory, acorn, cattail and wild sweet potato were obliterated and beyond having any present benefit in aiding the nourishment of those who were in the shadow of his protection.

The principle crop, golden maize, was in tatters; no different from the rest. The Goddess of Corn had rebuffed their offering as he had known it would. Imaginary gods have no impact no matter the efforts made.

The stalks had grown less than knee high as was customary and had appeared strong and deep in color. The spring planting that had been ongoing at his arrival into Kakeobuk's skin was progressing beautifully.

Until, of course, the whirling and drenching storm proceeded to brutalize their staple, their secondary tended plants and their wild and untended plants.

Their corn sparkled for so many reasons. It provided critical sustenance. It was used as tender to trade for other looked-for items. And it had, uniquely, allowed for the concentration of the populace that became Cahokia. Reliance upon migration, hunting and gathering diminished as the reliance upon a fixed and bounteous food source increased.

The sparkle was now gone.

To experience the battering of this wonderful resource was painful. His heart actually constricted and clutched for a moment as he contemplated the mangled maize before him.

He ate it not but recognized its necessity to those that he loved and cherished.

He would not be the leader who saw the demise of his people; even if just a borrowed culture for a temporary period of time. He had found the customs minus sacrificial rituals, the industry and the creativity of Cahokia monumental. He loved these people and was determined to successfully reinstate this culture to its prior magnificence and dominance over the territory that it had once ruled.

He was their Great Eagle and he would exert all the power within him to see to their restoration!

He opened his eyes and drew in a firm and deep breath. He felt able. He felt renewed. He felt calm.

_____

CHAPTER 22

A BROTHER'S
REFLECTION AS WELL

There had not been a drop of rain since the sheets of water had vanished and the clouds had receded and then disappeared. The sun's orb was brilliant and the sky was absolutely without a wisp of white whatsoever. There was a haze that clung to the city and its margins. Some of that came from the fires moving and spreading smoky trails that burst from the piled high pyres dotted everywhere. Removing the storm hurled debris was occupying the attention of all able bodied people.

Kakeokoke was incapable of doing anything other than sighing constantly. He was trapped in his reflections of what should be going on if the city had not been torn apart and routine activities of daily living were parading before him. He wanted that normalcy so badly and bore the horrible changes in a welter of sadness and consternation.

His brother suffered but never had to witness any of the distressing details up close and in the light of day. As far as Kakeokoke was concerned, this constituted a huge difference. The priest only managed to check his sobs by the greatest of exertions.

What should be transpiring in this once wonderful city of his?

He had taken everyday life for granted until now.

What was the first thing that he observed when he came out and down from his priestly habitat atop the mound at his back?

Ah yes, he was always impacted by the unceasing energy of the young children who ran and played in and amongst clusters of the women cooking around the many open campfires. Many of these women mingled loosely and easily from burning flame to burning flame and much chatter and laughter was always overheard by him. The familiarity and comfort of that had grooved itself into his wellbeing deeply.

Other females were working their fields or sizeable gardens and tended to the hoeing of the precious maize that lay at their feet.

Wherever the tribal women went, the babies and toddlers went also. The babies were stationary in the soft leather pouches that were slung over the shoulders of the toiling or talking women.

It was very rare that any men found themselves in fields or gardens planting or clearing the ground for crops of any kind. Kakeobuk had demanded that be done that singular night as he had felt that imminent crop crisis was upon them. He had correctly diagnosed a crisis but had not solved the issue of which crisis exactly. He had intuited slow and lean growth of the golden kernels, not devastation by flood.

Kakeokoke well understood that Kakeobuk was in grief over his miscalculation.

A tear slid along the priest's skin surface as he drew back into the cocoon of the city's prior regularity.

The men typically were at work in separate, individual locations knocking stone against stone in order to create and manufacture work tools or weapon blades. The fragments of stone shot everywhere and littered the work perimeter.

Other men sat in small groups upon the earth shaping stone or bone pipes and rarely spoke to one another as they labored over their beloved objects.

He was able to perceive out of the screen of his memory, at a distance, potters manipulating their gathered green clay; cleaning, sifting and kneading it. Other potters were crafting fine cooking and ceremonial bowls, cups and fine figures to be left as decoration upon the hearth configuration, whatever that may be. Some managed the art of pit firing objects in a deeply dug recess lined with clay and firewood. This effort continued throughout the day.

Periodically, he recalled, teams of hunters as they crossed the large plazas with freshly killed wild deer or turkey clutched by one or many.

The turkeys were a marvelous creature for the Indians of Cahokia. Their skins were as delicate and durable as deer hides. They were tanned with their feathers intact. These were then transformed into long and beautiful feathered capes which substituted as rain gear too. These amazing capes were not worn by the commoner but exclusively by the chiefs, the chiefs' counselors, priests and shamans. In other words, only men of status wore them.

And males of all ages fished for catfish, sunfish and bass in the creeks that wiggled their way in irregular direction through the area just outside of the palisade walls.

Further beyond, in his mind, a band of people were assisting in the construction of a home.

It was a marvel to watch a new home come to completion out of the hands of industrious and knowledgeable people. The one he was imagining was a modest and square house. Tall posts delineated the corners with smaller poles placed in between. Then the roof timber were put in place and lashed overhead with leather thongs that were wetted and then shrank as they dried. They used bundles of rushes and cattails also for the same purpose. The roof was now secure.

Several young women briskly wove bendable alder, willow and hazel rods from side pole to side pole and thus formed the walls of the house. Miraculously, teenage boys followed the young women by spreading mud and clay on the interior and exterior walls to make an impenetrable surface.

He smiled the tiniest bit as he visualized the steady pace of the mound builders themselves. Groups of earth carriers plied new soil in sixty pound baskets on their backs to the mounds peak in order to refurbish the mound's firmness. They climbed up the steep sides of the temple and burial mounds repeatedly. They dug their dirt from the ponds that lay scattered in the vicinity of the great city. At the mound's flat peak, mound dancers stomped the new matter into the old and then flattened it with the aid of deer antlers that raked easily through it all.

These mound builders and dancers were young and fit and were so very crucial to the making of a culture that thrived and spread.

Oh how he lamented the absence of that simplicity.

He opened his eyes now and all that he saw was a community thrashed and severely humbled.

He prayed that Kakeobuk was mighty enough to resurrect what appeared to have been utterly destroyed.

CHAPTER 23

TRADE THE CORN

That Kakeobuk was pinned to midnight spaces and was unable to pursue his leadership role during the sun's strong presence frustrated him immensely. Because of that, much was performed in his stead by the sensitive priest and his brother, Kakeokoke.

The two had smoked their pipes together on the eve following the manly tear that had fallen down Kakeokoke's cheek and they had concluded certain issues. They had mutually decided that a foray into all of the territory was necessary and it was wiser having The Great Eagle near at hand to his people for moral and psychological support. It protected Kakeobuk also as he always had his dark chamber in his immediate proximity. Therefore, the priest was to doff his priestly robes and depart as soon as men and supplies were collected for the trip.

In Kakeokoke's absence the members of the Great Eagle priesthood were to rotate authority amongst each other day to day when their leader was unavailable. Governance and restoration of the city was to progress without missing a drumbeat.

It was commonly acknowledged once announced by Kakeobuk that his inability to tolerate light was a permanent condition. Not a priest questioned the authenticity of this. Their reverence for their chieftain was absolute. He was never doubted.

The purpose of the watery journey down the Mississippi River was to trade for goods that were suddenly scarce and sorely required by the citizens of Cahokia. The necessity of cementing bonds and assisting restoration in the outlying communities was also critical in the ultimate survival of the land after the storm had raged. And further, he would bring back any and all volunteers to his city that were not needed in their own locality.

Kakeobuk had opened up his wealth to his brother in order to guarantee success in the venture awaiting several very adventurous Indians. What was presented to the priest was a shockingly large amount of corn ears to be used in exchange for necessities. A full canoe was carefully loaded with these fresh ears; ears that were to be exchanged for all the larger necessities deemed significant by the team of sojourners.

This canoe was lashed securely so that all the golden kernels would remain intact. The generosity of Kakeobuk in doing this revealed his anxiety over the fundamental survival of his ruled-over terrain.

The canoes were cavernous and consisted of well hollowed timber, crafted meticulously by builders of long experience.

The rowers had done this since their adolescence. They were well muscled and so were competent in all aspects of wave and water.

The river had receded considerably from flood levels that had swamped the land in the immediate moments after the storm had vanished. The current was brisk but very manageable. The river was even gentle in several of the broader regions of the vast waterway.

It was time to depart. The rowers took their paddles and pushed away from the shore. The canoes shushed through the ripples of current smoothly. The sensation of gliding was so powerful that none of the individuals except the rowers had an inkling of movement except to see the stars change position in the sky.

Early morning was upon them and the horizon brightened. The shimmer of the stars above blinked out rapidly.

The supplies of corn in Cahokia were plentiful enough that there was only marginal loss in this effort to trade the corn for the critical items which included clothing, meats, utensils and pots for eating and storing of goods, arrowheads and other implements of war and hunting and tobacco. The pipes of the tribe had to be filled. That was the greatest of necessities. Kakeokoke laughed at this.

He saw the humor even when it was black and despairing.

They plied the river for the day. They stopped at several areas of ruined houses, gardens and fields still full of mud. The priest was very adept at negotiations and found that while his corn vanished, his supplies of all else built easily. They were very diligent in ensuring that the corn was not damaged as they had to pack everything into the one canoe. The men, and their numbers were increasing, filled the hollow of the first canoe tightly.

This went on for approximately a week downriver and then the same in return to Cahokia.

There were occasions to aid in the clearing of brush, the erection of homes and the passing of news from one small and isolated area to another.

When the cluster of men broke out their pipes around the comforting fires and they shared words and stories; then the genuine healing of the region occurred.

At one fireside, there was an exchange which was disturbing for the priest. It carried a weight that very much concerned Kakeokoke.

And, of course, it revolved around the very subject that he suspected would arise at some point. He had hoped that it would not rear its ugly head but he had known that the likelihood of that was miniscule. There had been whiplash and many were disgruntled over the pronouncement by their chieftain that there was to no longer be maiden sacrifice to the gods that many cherished intensively.

"What, priest, will Katcheena Mondawmin's wrath become now that she is not fed the blood that she has always demanded?

"This is not good! This flood may be the very beginning of the anger that we might face. The crops may wither! The ground may shake beneath our feet. The sun god may bake the land. Our skin might peel from our very bones.

"Is the sacrifice of a woman, groomed to accept her death so that her tribe might be the better for her willingness to die, not reasonable?"

This Indian spat on the ground in disgust.

The priest spoke. "My brother, Great Eagle, has seen the god of our triumph and that god is one. I will not question my brother as he is with vision that moves even beyond my own!

"Submit to his edict and you shall see that our brotherhood with this god will provide for an alliance with the land which will bring prosperity and harmony!"

The Indian farmer hissed out these words, "There are many who do not agree. Their wrath may be nearly as strong as that of the abandoned gods! You are fools."

And he rose from the light of the flame and strode into the shadows without a backward glance.

In spite of the progress made upon the land and structures of Cahokia upon their return, an unsettled sensation held close to the priest's breast.

CHAPTER 24

DOWNWARD JOURNEY

L ying next to Kakeobuk bathed in the moonlight made vivid by the darkness in their sacred chamber, Minkitooni placed her hand on Kakeobuk's chest and his trepidation was palpable in his quickened heartbeat and his shallow breathing. He was unsettled and found it difficult to overcome.

They didn't even need to converse with words. Her hand upon his chest told him in unspoken expressions of her love and concern for him. The way her palm rested over his left nipple, and then moved in a circular motion, barely touching the puckering flesh, allowed him the knowledge of her arousal for him.

The leather beneath them was warming and the aura around them had a deep eggplant purple glow. Minkitooni reached over with her right hand to bring his face closer to her own. Taking his face in her hands, she closed his eyes with her thumbs and blew gently on his closed lids. Kisses followed so tenderly.

Her thumbs continued the effleurage over his skin. She touched him ever so softly under his eyes, his cheeks and the back of her hand caressed the sides of his face and under his chin. Kisses continued to follow.

Minkitooni felt Kakeobuk begin to relax under the sensual contact of her fingers.

Their kisses were repetitively slow, soft and sensual. Kakeobuk would kiss Minkitooni's lips and then take her bottom lip gently between his teeth. Minkitooni mirrored his movements and they breathed into one another's mouths.

Minkitooni was stirred, yes, but her need for showing tender love outweighed her desire for wanton intertwining. She reached around him and caressed his muscular back and shoulder blades. She pressed her fingers into his flesh until she felt the tension begin to break and his muscles begin to relax under her touch.

Her left hand continued up near Kakeobuk's face, sensitively tracing over his features while her right hand roamed down the center of his back, drawing circles and patterns on his flesh. Kakeobuk's breathing was regular now, but deepening as his own heat had awakened.

He allowed Minkitooni to take the lead with their joining and gave himself entirely to her desires now.

Minkitooni's hand moved down further, back and forth, across his strong back. Her fingers naturally dipped down into his deep sacral dimples and stirred little circles there. Kakeobuk appeared to enjoy this as he moaned, his cock thickened and lengthened easily. He instinctively moved his hips towards her and his growing manhood found a nesting place at the apex of her thighs.

Her fingers continued their journey downward even more, dancing over the rounded firm hills of Kakeobuk's buttocks. They were so firm there; so strong. At the beginning of the separation of his buttocks, there was a subtly concave area of very smooth, hairless skin. Her finger was compelled to go there and massage that small place, over and over. He relaxed even more so, and his skin was awakened to another very sensitive spot on his flesh. His cock rose and stood on its own with this little touch that was aimed elsewhere on his body. And, when her finger found its way down the natural crevice between these two strong hills, it rested for a moment, and dipped in ever so slightly at the wrinkled opening there.

Kakeobuk's kisses gained urgency about them.

His buttocks relaxed and Minkitooni was able to caress down through the crevice and up to the sack that held his orbs of life giving elixir. Her hand cupped him and encased him as she applied light pressure there.

Kakeobuk moaned and moved against Minkitooni, and she felt the readiness of him wanting to enter her. She had other plans for a bit.

Still facing one another on their sides, Minkitooni scooted down until she came within kissing distance of Kakeobuk's swollen and very hot to the touch cock. She held the knobbed mushroom cap in her left hand and cupped his sack in her right hand, holding him firmly there.

She made her tongue broad and flat and began licking his cock left to right, starting with the tight tense spot below the flaring head, all the way down to the base. She licked back and forth repeatedly. Her saliva created the lubrication needed to let her tongue keep gliding easily over his rigid flesh.

The sensation made Kakeobuk rock back and forth with some jerking movement as well. His groans let her know that it would not be long before he spilled his seed if she continued this tongue painting upon him.

He wanted to be inside of his love when he reached the crescendo moment. He lifted her reluctantly from his cock even though the feelings were so deliciously welcome.

She turned away from him this time and presented herself to him on all fours.

She reached through her legs and guided him, dew drops spilling copiously from his cock's opening, into her wet and wanting vault. The fit was perfect once again and filled her snugly and deeply.

He began to thrust into her, into her, again and again. She loved the hardness of his strokes inside her ready vault now and her innate tenderness left her momentarily.

Minkitooni found her own center, her red and swollen jewel d let her fingers press, rub and spank the flesh there matching the unding from her lover.

She felt his cock beginning to vibrate within her, his own climax rawing close, so she rubbed herself faster and harder; bringing erself to that place of no return. It was so hot there! Her pulsations ocked her.

She cried out as his deepest thrusts and his steaming hot creamy elixir filled her up. His own spasms continued within her and the contractions of her muscles milked him of every drop.

This much needed release for each of them worked the magic that Minkitooni had intended. Kakeobuk, totally relaxed, stayed within her. He pulled her to him, arm around her waist, one hand on her breast, flicking a responding nipple and rolled them both onto their sides so that they spooned against one another. Then he began to drift into the repose so necessary to free his mind for a short while.

Minkitooni smiled sweetly to feel his warm slow breaths on the back of her neck and entered her own state of peaceful contentment.

CHAPTER 25

FORTUNATE WOMAN

When they roused and left their bed-sling many hours later, the moonlight beams remained plentiful.

Kakeobuk stretched, still behind his love, and he let his fangs glance gently over her nape. She shivered on being awakened in this fashion.

She rarely was so bold with her powerful companion but she spun her entire body in a blur and reached for his now removed and soft cock. She squeezed it tightly and then ran her long fingernails over his vulnerable flesh there, leaving the faintest of scratch marks.

His cock was firmed by her maneuver but warned as well.

He kissed her nape then, licked away any harm, where none had been intended anyhow, and she softly pumped his shaft.

It would have been easy just to stay in the chamber and disregard his community above, but surely the Chieftain, Kakeobuk, knew that there was much to be done for and with his people.

Kakeobuk and Minkitooni appeared together at the front portion of the highest mound. Kakeokoke had been awaiting his brother and had much to share with him.

Kakeobuk stroked Minkitooni's hair and placed his hands on her shoulders.

"You have knowledge of the one God that I speak. Take the words that your heart knows and share them with the maidens.

There will be no more sacrifices. I know that they will listen to you as you sit with them and tell them of the loving God."

She nodded in agreement and responded, "My love, Great Eagle watching over his people, I will do whatever I can to move the mountains of their minds for the good of all."

Kakeobuk kissed Minkitooni in the center of her forehead and bowed slightly as he turned to join Kakeokoke.

Minkitooni began her descent from the mound to go and meet with the maidens in the virgins' residence.

As she passed along the way towards her destination, she was observed by the people. Some had come to have a real affection for her, but others stepped away as she crossed in front of them, not knowing if this taller, golden haired, lighter skinned woman had anything to do with the gods' displeasure.

These people were wary and frightened; ready to hide at the merest hint of calamity or crisis.

Minkitooni announced her presence to the maidens and requested permission to enter. The young women all stood and stepped to the side, almost in unison. Wankala, who appeared to be the eldest of the maidens, stepped towards Minkitooni, and spoke for the others when she said, "As our leader's companion, you need no permission to enter our abode. Please come and join us. Make yourself comfortable among us."

"Much thanks. I wish to sit and speak with you a while, if I may."

"Please do. We are eager to hear what the companion of Kakeobuk will share with us!"

Just as on the pathway to the their residence, when some of the people stepped aside, now in the home of the virgins, there were ones who appeared frightened of Minkitooni. They felt threatened by her presence and were not sure how to react to her being so close to them physically.

Minkitooni was so different from them. Her golden hair was so long with curls yet. She had eyes the color of water and sky together. Her skin was very pale in comparison to theirs. They were motionless as they looked her over and waited for her to speak.

"Our Kakeobuk has proclaimed that there will be no more sacrifices of the maidens, of you. There is no need to sacrifice your lives to gods that do not exist."

Wide eyed young women sat around Minkitooni and drew breath in but did not exhale immediately.

Wankala spoke again for herself and the other women she presumed, "I am eager to learn how this can be? Over the rise of one moon, there are changes from the gods we worship daily, to one god who has created all and is watching over all? This knowledge I do not comprehend. If we continue to displease the gods, we shall surely endure their wrath and suffer increased punishment."

Minkitooni reached out her hand to take Wankala's hand. The other maidens watched as the two women touched palm to palm.

"This is my understanding of the one God. I have been taught and I believe through Kakeobuk as well that there is one God who created everything on mother earth. All of the creation was made in a motherly way with much love and care. We are made to love and be loved like our God. We do not have to destroy a maiden's life to appease our God. God loves that the young woman is here and can sustain new life within to carry on the creation. That pleases God much."

Three of the young women stood up quickly and clutched hands over their ears. This was in spite of Minkitooni's message that they were now to live out their lives.

"We cannot hear these words of untruth! The gods must hear this and be so displeased! Their anger will be felt immediately!"

They ran from the residence to the Eagle totem on the mound to worship and try to appease their gods, avoiding their wrath in the process.

Others in the home with Wankala and Minkitooni shook their heads and clustered closely together, too frightened to listen, too frightened to leave their residence.

Wankala however appeared eager to listen to Minkitooni explain about this one God. Wankala sat very close to Minkitooni and began to stroke the long golden locks falling about the shoulders of the ivory hued woman. She took out a comb made from bone, and asked Minkitooni if she might comb her hair.

"I would enjoy the comb flowing through my hair very much. I am sure that there are tangled places that are so unruly that you may help smooth and soften them."

Wankala groomed Minkitooni's hair and listened more to the story of the one God.

"As there are unruly places in the world of my hair, on mother earth there are places and people who can become unruly for one reason or another. Our God grooms us, removes the knots and whatever hurts us and provides opportunities for us to be better. God helps our earth to be stronger and more pleasing. Like a father, God can be stern when it is necessary, so that we listen. Yet our God holds us tightly and lovingly as well."

Putting down the comb, Wankala faced Minkitooni and smiled. Wide bright eyes and a nodding head told Minkitooni that Wankala understood even before the words escaped her lips.

"I feel your words in my heart. I believe that I am coming to know and understand this one God of whom you speak. This God is love and my heart is so open to that feeling. It was an honor at one time to think my life, struck down would help my people. But after I am dead, if the gods are displeased, what then? Would another life be taken? Then another? Just as our people have done for ages? I don't feel a presence of love in our life here with so many displeased gods. I feel nothing from them, actually. When you speak of the God that you know, I already feel loved. I want more!"

Minkitooni extended her arms to embrace Wankala.

"This feeling of love comes from God. God gives us the gift of love and wants us to share it. I am so pleased that you understand the simplicity and wonder of it all. It is love. Come now! Let us go to Kakeobuk and share with him this triumph for you! Finding one person, and a young woman, a maiden such as you are, to understand and accept God, brings much hope to this people."

"We are going to the Chieftain, going to Kakeobuk? I have seen him from afar, but never have I been near to him. What will I do? What will I say?"

Minkitooni laughed. "Kakeobuk is a wondrous being. And it is also high time that he met the likes of you, Wankala. I am sure it will be an honor for him to set eyes on you, my friend.

"Gather just what you need for a few days and let us hurry; we don't want Kakeobuk worrying our absence any longer than necessary!"

"A few days, we are going to stay a few days with our Sachem?!" At that, Wankala dashed around gathering first and then holding in her arms what she would need for her stay with Kakeobuk.

Near breathless, she let Minkitooni know that she was ready to depart the virgins' residence.

Wankala actually led the way to the tallest mound where they expected to find Kakeobuk. Minkitooni chuckled to herself as she noticed that their footsteps were hurried.

Minkitooni spied Kakeobuk walking with Kakeokoke and looking quite serious in his conversation with his brother. They had been sitting and smoking the pipe for a while, then continued their words as they observed the community of their people.

Waving at Kakeobuk, Minkitooni motioned to him that she would like to approach him. He nodded and embraced his brother who then took his leave for the moment.

Wankala stayed close to Minkitooni's side as Kakeobuk came closer. He and Minkitooni embraced and he looked at Wankala who was gazing up at him. Wankala, though young and a maiden, had formed loving feelings towards him in her heart and mind. She shared this with no one as she had been expected to honor him by sacrificing her life. She was prepared to do so formerly, but now, she had God and Kakeobuk who was standing in front of her.

"Who is this tender, soft and sweet flower standing with you?"

Minkitooni bowed her head slightly, though Kakeobuk had always told her that it was unnecessary, and introduced her maiden friend.

"This is Wankala. I have brought her from the virgins' residence. She has heard the word of the one God and understands. She wants to learn more, much more!"

"Let me get a good look at this young woman who wants to know so much."

Wankala stepped forward and presented herself to her leader. She did not make eye contact with him for fear that she would faint. She was barely breathing at this moment. She had shiny black hair with the front sheared straight off right above her almost black almond shaped eyes. The lashes on those eyes were as long as the brown doe's lashes were. They were under thin yet lush black brows that made her eyes look even larger. Unlike the aquiline nose others possessed, Wankala's was thin, but slightly upturned at the end. Her lips were full and the color of red lilies that bloomed by day on the river bank. She wore a thin leather sheath, belted with beads and shells. Her feet were bare.

Wankala bowed her head but Kakeobuk lifted her chin to look at him. He embraced her and bestowed a kiss on her forehead. Wankala nearly swooned at that very instant.

"Kakeobuk, I have planned for Wankala to stay with us for a few days to gain more knowledge to share with the maidens and other members of the tribe. Does this please you?"

"This pleases me amply." Kakeobuk smiled.

Knowing that Wankala could not stay in their underground chamber with them, Kakeobuk and Minkitooni had her settle in one of the small homes used for the newly blessed couples of the fertility ceremonies. It was cozy, yet had enough room for all three of them to be contentedly together.

Minkitooni had food brought to them and treated Wankala graciously. Kakeobuk was sharing the rich information that he learned about the one true God.

Wankala was so open and appeared to soak up all his words like an ocean sponge. She sat at his feet but he lifted her to sit next to him so that their eye contact could continue in a more equal manner.

Time passed so quickly that Kakeobuk and Minkitooni nearly missed the first signs of an approaching dawn.

"As you know, I can no longer tolerate the sun. I must take my leave and go now. Minkitooni will join me. Please, dear sweet flower, Wankala, take time for rest yourself. Then, find one friend with which to share the news of God which I have just shared with you here. One by one, the people who have not yet relented will accept God as you have today. And knowledge of God will grow here in Cahokia. Minkitooni and I will return to you here after the sun has left the earth again."

Kakeobuk, the entity within, was always attempting to please his one and only master.

"I will rest as you request. I will share as you direct me Great Eagle. And, most assuredly, I will be here upon your return. Good rest to you and to the lovely Minkitooni."

Both Minkitooni and Kakeobuk embraced Wankala and each placed a kiss on her forehead and then her cheeks. Her cheeks were flushed and heated. Her heart was beating to the drums, to be with her chieftain and his companion. How fortunate a young woman she was.

CHAPTER 26

GIFT OF LIFE

They continued the conversation, the teaching and the laughter of getting to know one another for two days. On the third day, Kakeobuk approached Wankala with an idea that he had disclosed to Minkitooni in private.

"I have a proposal to make to you, sweet one. This is a proposal that will allow you to have pleasure and will equally provide you an opportunity to help our people at the same time. If you accept our invitation we will take you into our relationship and make you one with us.

"My first and foremost relationship is with my love Minkitooni. But she has suggested this union to give you the gift of first love; to take your virginity so that you would experience love and acceptance in the flesh. Sacrifices are no longer permitted. Were anyone to attempt that with you, both by law now, and the change in your flesh, they would be wrong, so very wrong!

"There may even be the gift of life to carry on the people of Cahokia. Are you willing to accept this gift, Wankala? It is offered with all sincerity. We have come to love you already and want you to have the best of everything."

Wankala's eyes glowed with anticipation at the thought of being with her indomitable chieftain and his companion in such an intimate way. She had never been with any man, as she prepared to give her life in sacrifice for her people. Now, she could give life to her people. What a wonderfully new way to please God and all else.

"Yes! Yes! I want to be a part of this union. I love you my Kakeobuk. I love you as well, Minkitooni. I will be with you as you desire. The wish has been in my heart for some time. Please lead me to the love that you share and give to me that gift that comes with that love."

Kakeobuk and Minkitooni knew from their special knowledge that Wankala would agree, so they had prepared the bed area in advance. There was honeycomb, a jug of tiswin, and flowers that had been placed all around. Oil from the maize, fragranced with sweet herbs, was also close at hand.

The room was softly lit with lamps. They led Wankala to the bed. Minkitooni reclined on the bed and patted a place next to her. Kakeobuk joined Minkitooni and then he in turn touched a place next to him and nodded to Wankala. She blushed a deep rose color and joined him on this generous bed.

Both Minkitooni and Kakeobuk embraced Wankala and kissed her. The couple shared kisses, showing Wankala in the gentlest manner how to join lips and swirl tongues. She was an adept learner. Her kisses, sweetened by the tiswin, were returned freely to Kakeobuk and Minkitooni.

Kakeobuk took some of the honeycomb and pressed it against Wankala's lips. The amber sweet thick liquid oozed from the comb and coated her full lips. He tipped his head towards Minkitooni who then leaned over to kiss Wankala's lips. The honey was so sweet as she licked it off. What clung to her lips after, she kissed onto Kakeobuk's lips as well.

The kissing of the lips, hands, necks and arms continued. Wankala was being awakened to all the sensitive spots on her womanly body. She, in turn, embraced and caressed and kissed her burgeoning and fascinating lovers.

Clothing became an encumbrance and soon Minkitooni was removing her sheath, exposing her elongated breasts with her lengthy, thick nipples. The coolness of the night air that crept in touched those nipples and they gathered and contracted, making them fuller and deeper in her wonderful raspberry hue.

Wankala felt so free that she removed her thin leather sheath and crawled between Kakeobuk and Minkitooni. Her young breasts were smaller and firmer to touch. She had never borne children, so her nipples and aureoles were somewhat dwarfed in comparison to Minkitooni's. Kakeobuk noticed their color; the shade of grapes that ripened on the vine in the autumn season. They were a very vivid purple red color. They made him hungry for the plucking and tasting.

Kakeobuk's member responded to this sight immediately. He had already risen in length and girth, but now the flaring and intensifying of his own color began. He removed his clothing and all three reveling in their bed had skin touching skin; differing shades of skin, varying temperatures of skin, but all responding to the loving touch from each other.

Their movements caused them to be only partially covered with a thin colorful woven cloth.

Minkitooni told Wankala how she liked to be touched on her breasts, and invited Wankala to touch herself and feel the sensations produced by caressing with the palms and the fingertips gently over that skin's surface.

Wankala closed her eyes to absorb every nuance of the touching. She reached over to touch Minkitooni to see if she felt any different than herself, and then she reached over to touch Kakeobuk's nipples to feel what a man felt like. His nipples responded to her touch, hardening into tiny pebbles.

"They are so hard! I want to touch them some more."

"That would give me great pleasure," sighed Kakeobuk. "Let me do this first, my sweet one."

He lifted one of her firm breasts to his lips and teased her nipple with his tongue. She moaned, yet watched him pleasure her this way.

"What I am doing to you, I enjoy having done to me. Minkitooni loves all of this too."

He reached over to pull his first love closer to him and raised her up to be on top of him. Her nipples were just above his mouth, and he opened his lips as she lowered herself to rest her jutting nipple on his waiting tongue. Minkitooni's nipple expanded steadily more and reached further with his tongue's contact. Then she replaced the first nipple with the second quivering fingerling of her flesh.

Wankala was touching her own nipples and leaned up to flick her tongue across Kakeobuk's chest now. The noises emitted from each of them were in a harmony of pleasure.

The excitement was growing in the three of them. Kakeobuk's was visibly so, nudging Minkitooni strongly at her soft belly as she maintained her position over him.

Minkitooni pushed down the cloth revealing the lower half of their bodies. Her mound was covered in reddish blonde soft curls, her nether lips were thin and that exposed her reddened jewel within. Wankala had lived with the maidens for a long time, so she had been familiar seeing other women, but Minkitooni's pale body just fascinated her and she had to look again and again. Her own body had black tightly curled soft hair covering her mound. Her nether lips were wide and closed over her tiny but powerfully sensitive jewel hidden from view.

Kakeobuk's proud cock rose to greet the women with its long shaft and flaring head. He touched himself and silently invited the women to touch him too. Minkitooni showed Wankala how to stroke him on that underside area. She used the pad of her thumb to stroke from the tight place down to the base. There was so much for Wankala to experience that Minkitooni did not use her tongue on Kakeobuk at this time. There would be plenty of time for other lessons on loving. This lesson was moving along quite well.

Wankala was a natural at lovemaking and learned the kissing and caressing and the stroking that would bring pleasure to herself and to her future partner. She reached down between her legs as she felt a twitching, almost an itch to be scratched there. Her clitoris, her jewel, had grown and was now protruding from its covering and throbbed to be touched. When she touched herself there, she jumped. It felt as if a shock had sped throughout her body. She was wet and glistened with a coating of dew she had formed in her vault.

Minkitooni and Kakeobuk kissed over and over and shared kisses with Wankala. Their moaning was getting louder and their breathing more shallow and rapid. It was time for joining.

Minkitooni, who was still atop Kakeobuk, raised her hips and she spread her nether lips with her hand. She was so ready for her lover to enter her. He was so ready to take her. His cock stood up straight and commanded her to settle upon it. Minkitooni lowered herself slowly and deeply onto Kakeobuk's cock. Wankala watched as their bodies moved together and instinctively began to touch herself. Her hands roamed around to find the greatest spot of pleasure.

She was rubbing her palm around her mons area and enjoyed the feeling of the flat of her palm against her moist flesh. She touched the nubbin that jutted out and it caused her to flinch in pain-pleasure when she hit the right spot. Her fingers worked their way to her opening. She was very tight there. She didn't know if she could take Kakeobuk into her with his massive size.

Minkitooni was moving faster and faster, getting closer and closer to her climax. She pinched her own nipples as she moved up and down on Kakeobuk, who writhed underneath her and held her hips. Minkitooni cried out as she began to reach her crescendo and her body spasmed intensely while atop of her lover.

Kakeobuk maintained such control, not spilling his seed. He had to have Minkitooni first, but he was saving his seed to spill into Wankala in hopes of creating a new life.

Minkitooni was fascinated as she observed her lover part the glistening fount that Wankala's opening had become. The maiden writhed on his organ and she needed no coaxing or teaching now.

Minkitooni simply whispered, "Hold still and let him stretch you slowly. The pleasure will outlast the pain in that way."

Wankala trembled as Kakeobuk paced his insertion into her carefully. She was a virgin, very tight with a maidenhead just split and trusted him at this moment with her sexual life.

He found her tunnel's bottom and held there. He nibbled on her nipples while she trembled thoroughly but did not move a muscle. He was her guide and she relied on that.

He was faint with his own restraint and the still posture of both enveloped them with a newfound sensation that was vast and complete. He shuddered and then massive bolts of his come pounded her insides. She was without prior knowledge of an orgasm and she snapped forward with her forehead to his chest. Her one and only cry was shrill and piercing. The waves that gripped her were fierce. She moaned over and over as his load continued.

Minkitooni was taken with this display. All were panting and ecstatic, ready for tension to dissipate.

If child had not been induced here, Wankala would never be of child.

CHAPTER 27

SHAMAN'S SMUDGE

S moke trails curled throughout the priest's prayer hut. The action of the burning herbs was purifying the space around him, opening the synapses of his brain and allowing him to journey into murky realms of spirits, ancestors and gods. He was not priest in this moment but, instead, he was shaman and his sweet sedge refreshed his proximate surroundings, his pinion cast the function of his mind into eccentric and less tangible forms and, finally, his juniper brought his vision to objects and places of clairvoyance.

Kakeokoke inhaled fully and drew the scents into and through his lungs to penetrate all of his internal organs, all the physiologic mechanisms that, in concert, forced his thoughts and senses out into regions sought by many but found by few. He was one of those few.

He was adept at divining the answer to significant questions via this transcendent route. He rarely used the ritual of spirit travel but had to ascertain the answer to the cessation of maiden sacrifice upon the future of his beloved city and people.

He had been fundamentally shaken when confronted with the angry and menacing response of the outlier, the Indian farmer, who detested Kakeobuk's proclamation. This priest, this momentary shaman, had naively assumed that all must follow the rules established by the Great Eagle. He was obviously wrong and was going in search of answers and restorative omens.

He knew not what he was to experience and find in the hallucinogenic endeavor he was initiating. He had to go and do this though as he felt the necessity of safeguarding citizens, Cahokia, the religion of which he was intimately bound even as it transformed itself and the widespread culture of the river's bottoms.

He forced himself to concentrate until, out of the swirling and multicolored images that flared, winked and then reformed chaotically within his skull, his animal guide took shape. His guardian totem had always been the massive brown bear. It was this shape or its growl that his very receptive senses sought.

There was a fist of white suddenly that shifted to what amounted to a curtain of the same color. He saw and heard nothing. The bear, his ally, always appeared eventually with the man's patience that combined both alertness and calmness.

He heard its padding paws before anything else. Then he perceived the black and moist snout separating the seam of endless layers of opaque white. The shaggy brown head and bulky brown covered body floated into visibility. The beast gently swung his head to the right and then to the left. His ears were extended and poised. And he ceased the movement of a sudden. The bear took in a breath and then, at length, stood stock still.

The man's sparkling inner essence was aware that it was now that the animal guide was ready to lead. A union was formed and the man relaxed into the comfort of the bond. Visions certainly must follow and flow.

The web of dull light grey mist parted grudgingly for the travelers. And it even seemed sticky often and thoroughly difficult to make their way through. It sucked the atmosphere into it and suffocated the two.

As they labored to find air for their starving lungs, the mists brightened, softened and appeared to fall back some. Inhalations eased and progress was made with greater surety. The bear's ribs rose and fell in a more effortless manner. The trudging turned into flight and they reached through the curtain to an elevation that revealed the huge orb of the sun and its potent and shimmering rays.

In this moment it was no longer the absence of air but the accumulation of heat that transfixed them and forced their best sight to be that of waves of shapes that eluded their ability to define. The paths of those golden beams were so simple to pursue and pursue them they did. The shapes approached, steadied and readied themselves for identification.

The most apparent of these shapes was the bosom of a long dark haired woman held stationary by something unseen. As their vision neared her nakedness, the woman's head dropped chin to chest as if the sinews of the neck had no strength remaining. The eyelashes fluttered as might a cluster of reeds sway in a summer breeze; back and forth waveringly, uncertainly.

The eyelids shot open and the irises were as black as the pupils. The white of the eyeballs exploded with the tiny bright red lines of bursting capillaries that were hemorrhaging at the horror of what they beheld.

In this very instant, the spear of sunlight exploded in and upon the mid forehead of the woman exposed to the seeker of the future and his guardian beast and a conflagration of flame erupted from her flesh. She did not disintegrate, rather she quaked briefly and then all of her skin peeled away from her bones in a charred black sheet.

There was nothing left of her to view after the briefest of time.

The space that her body had consumed was empty and dark.

The searchers were dragged through this hole, this pit, so rapidly that it was as if they had not moved through it at all. One moment they were perched at its entrance, the next moment they were pinned to the other side.

The sweeping landscape there was glowing and vivid but so far away. There was a quiet to the scene that was deeply unsettling.

Motion was at a minimum. In fact, they detected no movement of any kind.

All receded and he and his guardian vibrated and did not stop. It went on for an unknown length of time. He and the bear elongated little by little and became shapeless.

As the vibration ceased, Kakeokoke felt a returning thud of consciousness. He was awake and drowsily aware.

Time passed and he regained his mental equilibrium.

He recognized that the future was thick with uncertainty and cheerless possibilities.

And he further discerned that the sacrifice of the virgin maidens had no impact on Cahokia's outcome whatsoever.

How did he know this? The sun's rays would have formed arrows that shot into the woman's body if the sacrifice of the virgin maidens had been significant. But they hadn't.

CHAPTER 28

REBEL'S REVENGE

S he despised the purity and inexperience of the young women who would dwell in the residence of the virgins briefly longer. Shortly they would be moved. To her, they were too foolish and naïve to waste further time and energy on.

And for that, all qualities of which she was not, she had been convinced without difficulty by Mikilenia to perform this deed.

He had demanded it because he bristled to reveal his power and yearned to eliminate that which was loved by his enemies as Wankala was loved. Any other deaths were simply collateral damage and not worthy of concern.

Anteekwa had promised him it's doing and he in return promised her the gift of immortality. If she failed at this they were only to be lovers, no more, no less. He would perpetually refuse her the dark benefits of the undead.

She feared aging. And now that she had discovered the perfect partner for her, she was grossly frightened of growing old, infirm and unattractive while he maintained his beautiful being throughout her changes.

She was desperate for success here and brought her torch down to the first of the four corner wood posts supporting the structure. These posts were never clay or mud daubed and so provided the perfect wick for the flames destructive powers to rip and burn.

She knew how to sprint with her body compressed at half her ordinary height and had four pockets of fire smoldering at the exposed posts quickly. In only minutes, the smoke seeped into and then filled the inner sanctum of the residence.

Two final acts had to be accomplished by her before she sped away. She tossed the lightweight torch onto the thatched and wood woven roof.

She had located a log large enough to block a door but small enough for her to carry before she had even lit her torch. She brought the fir round to the only opening that the building had. She wedged it tightly against the door's center and kicked the second end until it dug deeply into the ground.

No one would depart alive, Anteekwa was sure.

The smoke billowed into the interior now and the roof was completely ablaze. The escalating cries, then screams of the young maidens became shrill and horror filled. Wankala, her last intended night spent in this shelter with her sisters of the sacrifice became the last night of her life. Whether she had been impregnated by Kakeobuk no longer mattered. Her wails blended frightfully with the cacophony of the rest. The sound of the red, blue and yellow engulfed timber's crackling soon overwhelmed any human noise from the interior.

Anteekwa fled as quickly as she had arrived. Her footfalls were not heard by the oncoming Kakeobuk, Minkitooni, Mahkwa and Ashkipaki as they rushed as close to the scene as their undead flesh allowed them. They were unable to be effective in any way regarding the fire.

Kakeokoke and his priestly seconds hastened to the scene as well.

The fact that the virgins' residence was considered a sacred space meant that it had been placed atop the very mound that Kakeobuk's dwelling and the temple inhabited by the priests had been established. Even that proximity saved not a single woman caught inside the inferno that lashed at everything in its path.

No other structures were located close enough to be at risk from the spread of what appeared to be an accidental tragedy.

Kakeobuk wept as they realized that their Wankala had been inside and that the fire had swallowed her whole. Kakeobuk gnashed his teeth, fangs gleaming as he did this, and groaned, "Why was I not able to see this coming?! Where was my mind?!"

Minkitooni wept as well for her newly found friend and kindred spirit. Had Wankala lived into the days to come, either the Great Eagle or his pale undead companion would have nourished Wankala with the very gift that Anteekwa was receiving from her lover and rebel of revenge, her Mikilenia.

The heat was atrocious and there was little that anyone could do for the dead women.

The fire consumed its fuel completely and then, when there was no more of that to feed upon, the flames flickered out. There were embers lighting up the surroundings still and ash floated everywhere.

Kakeokoke pondered, as the tears upon his cheeks evaporated from the intense heat that he ignored, whether this was what the black sheets of skin that peeled from his hallucinogenic woman signified. Had he been told of this calamity from his vision?

If so, there was only ash that swirled in the lingering currents of air here. No sheets of black skin existed. All human remnants had been immolated and had disintegrated into nothing more than fragile flakes of ash. What of that?

He found this conundrum impossible to solve. He had been guided to the future by what he had seen but there was nothing that told him precisely how to interpret the happenings, shapes and colors that had tormented him as his bear totem stood at his side. The reality of the pictures that had pinged off his skull were elusive and not coming clear for him now.

This had never happened to him before. He was master of discernment when it came to interpreting spirit messages. He was racked with sadness and confusion by the perils that were fast approaching Cahokia.

He fisted the sides of his head and squeezed as if that might bring some kind of clarity to his dazed mind.

He lurched back to his temple accommodations and his priest brothers followed.

He was stymied and he felt that if answers were not produced rapidly, end times might be very near at hand.

He thought of his beloved sibling and was even uncertain of the power of the Great Eagle to rescue their once mighty civilization.

CHAPTER 29

URGENT GROWLS

This was another promise that Anteekwa affirmed as she and Mikilenia lay in one of the deeper horizontal and mildly descending shafts that bled from the mine's core. The flood had not ravaged this tunnel and what wet had seeped in slowly evaporated. There was a naturally carved ledge at tunnel's closed end that they used while in undead slumber. She, of course, was able to sleep anytime but she chose the same hours of her lover's repose.

And what promise had she made him? She would do anything to be turned and he knew that. He only used this knowledge to manipulate her some. His feelings for her restrained him from doing her true harm. It was his Minkitooni, his Aiobheean, whom he craved and loved but Anteekwa was lush and lovely and so he would accept her forever if necessary.

She had burned the maidens alive, Wankala being his actual target, and she was set to do his bidding once more.

"Yes, I will wear it always. I only do this for you love. I would not do this for anyone else."

Mikilenia had scoured the shops on the plaza for this object. He did not explain his actions to Anteekwa as she remained below ground. She did not have his powers yet and as he explained, her accompaniment would have been a hindrance to him. She complied out of her usual devotion to him.

He had entered these shops at night and surreptitiously as only a demon was capable. He needed no invitation. That notion was myth and fabrication. He went where evil had or did linger. Evil was within all humans. So he journeyed wherever humans journeyed.

It was a wasted search however as he found nothing that fit his imagination for her. If he discovered a likely object, he planned on pinning it to her flesh for the eternity that soon was to be hers as well as his. This was the promise she had given him, that she would permanently wear it in deference to his wishes.

As he returned to the temporarily abandoned workshop and mine he stumbled upon the perfect metallic object of his search. It had been one of many scattered across one of the artisan's tabletops. The designs varied slightly and this one was, by far, the best for his purposes.

It was tiny. The copper had been formed into an almost flawlessly round ring. The ring's band was thin but, as he rolled it over repeatedly in his hands, he discerned its genuine strength.

The supremely marvelous aspect of this ring was not its extraordinary luminosity or that the partially finished aspect accentuated the thoroughly frightening design. No, the special quality was in the configuration, the shape, of what was contained within the center of the circle. It was ideal and would transfix and cow all who beheld it upon her exposed nipple. The bulging head, the threatening eyes and the scimitar-like length of the fangs of the coiled and ready to strike serpent even brought eerie prickles to the back of his neck.

Anteekwa loved the trinket immediately.

Mikilenia spoke to her softly but stared firmly into her eyes. "We will find our bliss now. While we pleasure one another, I will blindfold you so that you will not observe and will undergo increased sensation as all of your other senses will be enlarged to compensate.

"There will be pain as I will bite one of your nipples and place the uppermost portion of the band into your skin. It will hang from that rent flesh of yours. Once, though, after I have rendered you immortal, your nipple will heal instantly around the copper and you will never feel pain or infection from it after.

"And I impale it upon you when you are human so that you will be scarred forever in the memory of the intensity of our union!

"You, as vampire then, could remove it and heal fully. But if you ever do that, you will never see me again."

Anteekwa was so desirous of his play upon her that she nearly panted out, "Yes, my god, yes, Mikilenia! Stop the words! Do it now!"

He continued with only these, "Your nipple, and I chose the left one, huge as it already is must become larger to fit the band precisely.

"I will kiss you there first."

She had bared both breasts to him before he had completed his last sentence. When he bent his head to her, she offered up what was already a long and dark nipple to him.

Even without his elaborate plans, he sucked on her thick and raven tip as if he were famished. Anteekwa moaned feverishly as her senses were so wanton.

It was at this moment that he situated the folded small cloth over her hair and her eyes. She trembled at the placement of this blindfold upon her and unconsciously tightened and released her thighs in her heat. She was a gushing flood of liquid down there in spite of comprehending her very imminent pain.

He lanced the gorgeous and now doubly swollen nipple so delicately with one of his scalpel-sharp fangs. He sheared only enough of the topside of her utterly sensitive flesh there, licked away all of her oozing blood and squeezed the separated skin together around the fierce copper talisman, lifted his head to her lower neck and sank deeply into her buttery soft flesh. Her carotid, what he sought, was found.

She moaned, quivered, jerked and jumped minutely in the dual feeling of it all. The pain predominated initially but then she swooned into the pleasure of his taking draughts of her precious crimson fluid. She seized sweetly as she fell into his fang's embrace.

He pulled away from her then and observed her nipple seamlessly close around the beautiful ornament.

He had passed the gift to her and she was his undead partner indefinitely.

He, though, had not slaked his thirst. Neither had she.

He raised her doeskin skirt, she spread her legs for him gladly and he mounted her with shaft huge and at the ready. They joined with hips slashing together. She cried gutturally as she felt her orgasm. He then poured his pearly juices into her, spurt after spurt.

Only then did his urgent growls dissipate.

CHAPTER 30

Flight of Mind

The four sat in a circle upon the floor's surface within their chamber and they listened to Kakeobuk intently.

With their acute hearing, they also listened to the saddest but sweetest of mournful music that seeped through the mounded walls to them. It must have been the paean sung by Indian relatives in their anguish over the tragedy of the young virginal women. It was to take a long period for there to be recovery from that event.

"Kakeokoke told me this story and I will reveal it to you.

It moves me as I feel the same qualities of this fable within the tribe that resides here."

He began, from memory, the rendering of the so sensitive birth of corn amongst the Indians.

"In ancient times, a humble widowed Indian woman was dwelling with her children in a beautiful part of the country. She was further humbled by the fact that she was unskilled in finding food for her family and in that her children were young yet and unable to assist her. In spite of these minimal skills and hard circumstances, she remained of a kind and contented disposition. She was so thankful to the gods for all that she managed to gather together. Her eldest daughter was gifted in the same gentle manner and she had now reached the age where the ceremony of Ke-ig-uish-im-o-win, or fast, occurred. In her fasting, she would find her spirit guide and guardian through her life.

"This young woman, Wenona, had been dutiful since the moment she grew old enough to help her mother and was much cherished by her whole family. As soon as this particular spring season gave arrival's indication, the customary tiny lodge, at a distance from their primary abode, was built. She was not to be disturbed as she performed her solemn rite.

"She prepared herself and went immediately into this little hut and began her trial without food. In the beginning, she amused herself by walking the area and observed the plants and flowers that existed in abundance there. This was done as she wanted to settle into dreams that were peaceful and pleasant at her hour of sleep.

"As she wandered, she felt a great desire to become more aware of how the plants grew without man's aid and how some were good to eat and some were poisonous and harmful. These wonderings came to her mind after her trek and she was now too tired to do more. She had confined herself to the lodge for the moment, was lying down and pleasantly resting, hoping for ideas to come to her as to how she might be of service to her family.

"One thought that predominated was this, 'True that the Great Spirit makes all things and it is to that Spirit that we owe our lives. But might we be blessed by being able to find our food easier than by hunting animals and taking fish? I must try and find the way in my visions!'

"On the third day, she became more weak and faint. She was unable to move from her bed. While in this position, she observed a striking woman come down from the sky and advance towards her. This woman was handsomely and brightly dressed; her garments were of lighter shades of green and yellow. The plume upon her head was beautiful and every movement that this woman took was assured and graceful.

"The otherworldly visitor softly intoned, 'I am sent to you, my friend, by that Great Spirit who makes all things of the sky and earth. Your motives in this fasting are known therefore. Because your wish to do good for people is at the heart of what you seek, I am sent here to instruct and reveal to you how to do your people well.'

"She followed by telling Wenona to rise up and to prepare to make heavenly music on the flute with her as this was the only method that she might succeed in her wish being granted. Wenona had never played the flute before. She did know where to place her lips but not how to cover the openings of the instrument to create sweet sounds. She felt wan and weak but suddenly felt her song of songs surging in her heart. She got up, took hold of the flute handed to her and with much effort played many notes that were barely connected. The spirit wraith smiled and told Wenona that it was enough for this moment and then disappeared completely.

"It was the fourth day and Wenona anticipated the return of her vision. She was not disappointed. Wenona was even frailer now but the trial was renewed immediately. The weary young woman produced the softest of notes before the stranger added, 'Tomorrow will be your last trial. Be of strong faith and you will overcome me and find your way to the boon that you seek.'

"In Wenona's dreams that eve, birds flocked to her shoulders, touched her neck and found tree branches everywhere to sing to her. Their songs were lodged in her heart, mind and fingers now.

"The next trial, Wenona played the flute and it called to the sun, the clouds, the rain and the rainbow. It called the many animals from the surrounding woods to sit and listen in keen attention at the forest's edge. The songs of the flute that Wenona brought forth were powerful in spite of her fading energy. She was determined to prevail or perish in the effort. She used all within her and after the contest had lasted its regular length the stranger ceased her efforts and declared herself conquered. She whispered instructions in Wenona's ears as to how to collect her hard earned and well-deserved gift.

"The next day, the last one of her fast, Wenona followed the stranger's instructions exactly as she had been told. And everything happened exactly as the stranger had said.

"On that morning of the seventh day, Wenona's mother came with light refreshments of food and liquid saying, 'My daughter, the fast is accomplished. If the Great Spirit will favor you, it will be done now. You are to restore your strength as the Master of Life does not require you to make the ultimate sacrifice.'

"Wenona replied, 'My mother, wait until the sun goes down. I have a particular reason for extending my fast to that hour.'

"The older woman told her that she would wait.

"At the ripe and routine hour, the sky-visitor returned and she and Wenona produced song from their instruments. Wenona played her angelic flute with such beauty and charm that the widow spider arrived exactly as had been mentioned in the instructions. The black spider climbed to the visitor's neck and with the slightest of bites drained away her life swiftly. Wenona lowered her to the ground and, upon finding her spirit gone and her body dead, removed her wondrous garments and instantly buried her on the spot. She took all precautions that she had been told of and was very confident that this friend was to come again to life eventually. The grave of her friend was remembered always.

"Wenona visited this site throughout the spring, weeded out the grass and left the ground in a soft and pliant state. Soon, she saw the tops of the green plumes coming up out of the earth's surface. The more she tended this ground, the faster they grew. Weeks passed in this fashion.

"The summer was ready to exit when, one day, Wenona invited her mother to visit the tended ground with her. It was where the lodge of her fasting had been but was now removed. In the lodge's place there stood a tall and graceful plant instead. This plant had bright-colored silken hair, topped with nodding plumes and proud leaves with golden clusters on each side.

"Wenona cried, 'It is my friend and the friend of all creatures. It is Mondawmin. Planting will go hand in hand with hunting and fishing to aid in our success. If we take care of the land, the land will give us a bounty year in and year out.

"This is what my fast was about.

"The broad husks must be torn away as I did thus in pulling off Mondawmin's garments for her proper burial. Once having torn away the husks, one must hold the ear toward the fire until the outer skin becomes brown and still the milk is retained in the grain.'

"The entire family united in a feast that was supplied by the wonderful resilience of Wenona, the sweet grace of Mondawmin and the deep patience of the Indians who now benefitted from the gift of the gods.

"Wenona and her mother embraced and spilled tears in their embracing."

Upon Kakeobuk's telling of this tale, this flight of the mind that was lovely and good, so like most of what they viewed of this culture, Minkitooni and Ashkipaki wept openly. The two men held their women tightly and knew love.

The mournful sounds from the exterior of the chamber continued.

CHAPTER 31

TALISMAN'S TOUCH

Indian farmer after Indian farmer was so disgruntled, even indignant and very angry, at their Great Eagle's decision to put an end of sacrifices to their gods. Even though Kakeobuk was their leader, many an Indian felt that his actions were vastly insolent and that in his rebuke of the old deities, those very deities would rain punishment down upon them. And hadn't there been punishment enough already?

Mikilenia and Anteekwa, now that she was also undead, were intimately aware of the animosities that Kakeobuk's decision had aroused. And the headstrong pair was planning on taking advantage of this to aid them in usurping the current chieftain's power and authority and take it for their own use.

Mikilenia knew that he had completely lost his bearings after he realized that his life's love had given her allegiance to the swine, Kakeobuk, and his entity within. It was a maddening sore upon Mikilenia's psyche that no amount of scratching relieved his need to dig at it repeatedly. Even Anteekwa's obvious devotion to him, the attachment of such a beautiful creature, only covered the wound superficially and temporarily. If he was not to have Minkitooni, his once Aiobheean, he was going to make her life sheer and unrelenting hell if he could.

He comprehended that it was mad but it penetrated to his undead soul and this wayward behavior of his became ceaseless.

And they were participating in this reactive and rebellious behavior even now.

It was late into nightfall, easy campfires had been lit long ago by others, and they were gathering allies for his planned takeover of Cahokia. Part of his strategy was to persuade them to immediate action by stirring them through the potency of Anteekwa's words, demeanor and talisman. She was Indian, she was lush and she did his bidding passionately, alive or undead.

She spoke to these clustered men, their wives left behind as war was a man's preoccupation, and she was never shy or hesitant in their presence. She was princess and their magnet and compass. "Mondawmin will not be ignored! Believe me; she will use her serpent of punishment again. The god's serpents rule. The flood was just the beginning of how she will show her wrath to us!

"Follow us in unseating Kakeobuk and Mondawmin and her serpent will see to our perpetual success and we will return maidens sacrificed on our altar to her womb. She will have all the blood that she requires and then some!"

Mikilenia moved nearer to Anteekwa upon the closure of her invocation to action and hissed this, "I will expose Mondawmin's serpent in all its light and glory to you this very moment if you give me your pledge to cast Kakeobuk and his minion down immediately!"

The gathered individuals were as if in a trance from the flickering fire, the hot words and the anticipation of Mikilenia's promise to them. Almost in unison, those there and there were many, and many from prior campfires, hoarsely rasped out their "yeas" and automatically nodded their heads up and down.

Mikilenia brought his promise to them then. He slid behind Anteekwa and parted her deerskin tunic very slowly. Anteekwa sought this exposure and sat fully still. As the material separated from her chest more, the held breath of the male watchers was loud in its utter silence.

Then Mikilenia drew the material fully aside suddenly and her magnificent breasts bobbled heavily into view. The held breath turned into a collective gasp and then into a wavering exhalation of excitement. Pulses surged and members thickened.

Then Anteekwa caressed the upper curve of both breasts. She let her left hand fall to her ornamented nipple. Her other hand pressed into her flesh above her nipple with her palm to make the remainder of that breast and nipple prominent. And it had its desired effect on the stunned audience.

"Here is Mondawmin's serpent. It lies upon my nipple. It will feed you but you must feed it first. Make your pledge to it. Come one at a time and kiss the serpent upon me. Make it quiver and move to you. Feel its power on your tongue and your lips.

"Do it now!" Her command caused immediate compliance by all.

Mesmerized and desperate to follow through, but with respect for one another as well, they began to approach individually and very, very reverently. It was as if Anteekwa was the goddess herself. Was she? She seemed it. And even if she were not, her nipple left them incapable of doing other than to bow to the demand of her command!

Each and every capitulating male, which was all of them, had various degrees of throb and large tumescence upon them. The strength of the atmosphere, Anteekwa and Mondawmin's serpent riveted them to this moment.

The first arrived and kneeled at her dark tip and beautifully hung copper ornament. The talisman had touched him from a distance. He would touch it close at hand now. And he did.

His fingers gently stroked over the metallic surface to ensure its concreteness and reality. He pulled upon it slightly and then more forcefully over and over, hardly aware of his actions. Her nipple quivered, tensed and elongated towards him. Her Venus Mound gushed liquid then but that was invisible underneath the deerskin skirt that she continued to wear.

Mikilenia intoned, "Kiss the messenger of Mondawmin. Kiss the serpent! Kiss her nipple! Make it move. Firm it to show your desire to please the serpent and its master!"

The man avidly did just as Mikilenia said. He placed his lips to the gleaming object and then did the same to the hot, hard tip that made Anteekwa moan quietly but feverishly. She was unable to resist and pressed the man's head into her as he suckled her there.

Mikilenia then firmly, without harm or pain, pushed the face from her mountain of flesh. "Show her your cock and let her suck you there."

Again, he followed Mikilenia's instructions rapidly, and she held and then stroked his livid shaft as she hard sucked his cockhead. The sounds of the fusion of her gliding lips upon him hugely aroused all.

Simultaneously she fisted Mikilenia's rearing shaft with her other hand. He spread his legs for her; put his hands on his hips and his eyes glittered as he faced the audience. His loin cloth had long ago been pushed aside by his flushed and emboldened cock.

This fortunate Indian groaned deeply at her motions and shot his thick spurts deep into her throat. She took it all and swallowed it wantonly.

Mikilenia sent the spent man back to his place as Mikilenia's dew dripped copiously from her jack hammer strokes.

Anteekwa moaned some more. Her nipples thrived and she stroked herself. She was unable to keep her one hand away from the talisman as she pulled it all directions.

"We will not satisfy all of you tonight. We need your energy. We do promise you that we will follow through once we have become victorious over the city and hold its authority in our hands.

"Anteekwa begs for a few more so that she may come simply from her satisfying you. One by one won't do. I want you to know who your leader is. So I will pick you, you and you only."

He cast his pointing finger upon three further men. This was what it would take for Anteekwa to be satisfied. His prescience knew this.

The shapes of the first and then these next three cocks that she relished putting hand and tongue to escalated her until the final cock, long and of bulbous head, made her its captive as he burst thick spurt after thick spurt down her throat. She swallowed only the first eruptions and then let all see his looping arcs of come as she released him from her mouth. He pumped his own cock when she stopped to milk it all out completely.

With this, Mikilenia groaned deeply and looked at her hand and his own cock as she jerked him to an explosive ejaculation that sprayed repeated abundant white streams as the other Indians loosed themselves as well.

As the two males released, she finally fell into her own paroxysm of ecstasy. She leaned on her one backwardly extended arm where the ground gave her support, she moaned and panted in abandon while watching Mikilenia's jerking shaft and her hips tightened and seized as if a cock were thrusting inside of her vault. Her belly rippled and her release was gripping and then it freed her. She became so limp after. Her entire being felt soothed.

Mikilenia felt it all in addition. He did not need to touch her to crave her mounting desire and then her set of body waves that consumed her core.

White speckled the blades of grass.

CHAPTER 32

ROILING RAGE

A ll were so fused to their storming release that no one, Mikilenia too, was even remotely aware of the cessation of the beat of wings and a transformation of the four to their Indian form.

Earlier in their chamber, once the tale of the corn had been told, Minkitooni turned her tear stained countenance to her love and tremulously cried out to him, "How can you, feeling the exquisite potential of these people, let them be ruined by his pathetic tantrums? You, as we are not equal to you and never will be, are so much more powerful than he is and must fling him and his harlot from these regions. It must be done now!" There was no more wavering of her words as she gained momentum of the naturally righteous. And it was truly righteous because she did not think of herself at all.

Kakeobuk was shamed and let his passion to leave events to their own unfolding vanish. He allowed his outrage to escape into the open and it escalated into a roiling rage that forced him into immediate action.

Mahkwa and Ashkipaki were insistent with Minkitooni that Mikilenia's rebellion had to be ended one way or another without delay!

"We will accompany you Kakeobuk. It is, after all, my son's doing that brings us to this brink. Possibly, I might persuade him to do other than he is doing.

"We must go now though."

"I taught him once and I understand that there is a thread of decency within him. In addition, you, entity, aided him as he led a people primed to be birthed into a new nation. Assist him again!

"He truly requires that from you."

"I need no more convincing. Let us go to him in this hour and resolve what might have been better resolved some time ago!"

With that, they altered their shape, exploded from the mound, sought the sky and went to where numbers of individuals were massing against them.

Mikilenia had dropped his guard as the torrent of group ecstasy gripped him, Anteekwa and their participating audience. That was how the four discerned the location of this particular campfire. The scene did not make them reel in the slightest as they had become privy to his escapades at that moment of his weakness. Their seer powers did so much for them.

Kakeobuk touched ground first and shape shifted. The three others followed suit just barely after him. He was upon Mikilenia in several of his huge strides. He emerged from the shadows as an angry and avenging god would.

Kakeobuk grabbed the wayward brethren by the scruff of the neck, squeezed hard and easily lifted him into the air as if he were nothing more than a rag doll to be held up and disciplined before a crowd.

All writhing and motion from the Indian audience went absolutely still. Danger was acute and in their face.

Mahkwa, Minkitooni and Ashkipaki surrounded Anteekwa. The Indian who was involved with her orgasm went to softness so rapidly that his cock shrank and fell from his now palsied hand. He scurried away on all fours.

Mikilenia's trance and thrill were shattered.

Anteekwa's body did not shake the ebb of her release instantly but shortly thereafter she felt the definite presence of the three and the one.

The rebel undead hissed and lashed out with his arms flailing and his legs kicking backwards. Any contact that was made simply glanced off of Kakeobuk harmlessly. The entity within had nearly the power of the almighty. Or so it felt in this moment. Mikilenia's fangs and coaxing eyes were rendered useless upon Kakeobuk as he was compelled to look forward.

The Great Eagle shook the craven bastard over and over. The earth trembled beneath his feet as he did this. The ground even was quaking at the strength of the Indian leader.

Anteekwa observed this and the menacing expressions on the faces' of the three simultaneously. She submitted then and there. She simply desired that she and Mikilenia survive and escape.

"No more, Mikilenia! No more! Your tainted heart has riddled these people with hostility and urges of power and revenge. They are you and you are them! And that bond is ended, crushed, I say!"

Ashkipaki lanced her words towards her son. "You are my blood, Mikilenia. Woe that I must admit that but I must as it is the truth. You have the capacity because of that, because it is my capacity as well, to seek out the truth and let that truth quell your seething and damned impulses! Let those impulses pass. Find a better way."

A new voice was heard. "I taught you once, Mikilenia," Mahkwa reminded. "And you were wise and full then.

"Once, also, I saved you. You were never aware of that though. Let me save you once again. If you follow my words here, you will be aware that I have saved you this time.

"Let your jealousy go. Love this woman who obviously loves you. Be content with that and make peace with all that is offered you.

"Rise above the disappointment that I know is a hard knot in your gut. It can and must be done!"

Minkitooni simply jeered, "You my once liege lord are beyond disdain!"

Again it was Kakeobuk's turn. The flames of the dying campfire continued to flicker a bit longer. Mikilenia was motionless with his head hung down. Whether it was a ploy or a sincere humbling was difficult to figure as he blocked their tendrils of sight aggressively.

"Mahkwa has convinced me that you might redeem yourself and find a means of overcoming your vulgar recent actions.

"So, I am letting you free but am casting you from this territory at the same time. You will deeply regret it if you return.

"Go with those who will see you to your possibly better times.

"You will go now and do not make the mistake of finding yourself in or near Cahokia ever again!"

With that pronouncement, Kakeobuk placed Mikilenia back on ground's solid surface.

The dark swallowed him up as he, Anteekwa and a few of his Indian compatriots fled with him.

Mahkwa was wrong, though, about his once student.

CHAPTER 33

HUNTER'S PRAYER

He was a worrier by nature and let his mind take him back to the landscape of Cahokia in the recent shaman's travels. The landscape had been barren and empty; thoroughly so. This image happened to have coincided with the memory of words exchanged when he and his cohorts had gone downriver to trade their corn. He had quaked internally then but let the episode vanish in the tide of immediate needs. His remembrance now, especially having had the very foreboding vision, made him quake for a second time.

In that memory, coincidentally, as if he read the priest's mind, the young hunter who sat beside him asked a question that probed deeply as if with the sharpest knife wielded by the hush of the dead. They had worked the river, traded for many goods and were smoking pipe with a splendid tobacco leaf as they also enjoyed the good fire that lit the dark cleared spaces. The day had been hot and the night still warmed their skins. Yet the flame was calming, familiar and as if they were with a friend. The relaxation of the moment turned sharply away once the dialogue of queries began.

The first and only query from the usually extremely quiet and efficient young hunter, who on this venture substituted as a rower of great prowess, was a very legitimate question. This one then set off a chain reaction of queries back from Kakeokoke.

"I take no comfort in asking you this revered priest but I am compelled to do exactly that as my spirit finds little rest and contentment of late."

Kakeokoke puffed benignly on his pipe but churned inside from the tone of the inquiry. Regardless, he replied. "It would please me to be able to make your spirit peaceful and settled. Let me help if I am able.

"So speak your piece to me."

"Before the rains fell, before the flood soaked the ground and before our city was brought to her knees, we who hunted sensed the lessened abundance of animals to find and bring home to feed the many hungry stomachs of our people. This is to say nothing of the scarcity of the hides available for preparation and wearing.

"What have we done wrong?

"Find an answer, so that we may restore that abundance that was once much larger and more plentiful even in my lifetime."

With closed eyes and a deep sigh, Kakeokoke started his search for an answer.

"Did you perform a ceremony before you set forth?"

"Yes my teacher, I danced to my brown deer spirit and I heard the hymn of success through him. I wore the skin of the deer and his head covered my head. Other of my brothers wore the fur and head of the buffalo. I took my sacred animal stones to keep me close to those very creatures.

"We gave offerings to He-Who-Brings-Them-In and his visions were strong and clear. He accompanied us as well."

"And you followed the customs prescribed for a fortuitous outcome?"

"Yes again, leader here. We bathed early and dressed lightly for speed and silence. We wore nothing other than our clothes at our waist and upper legs. We left the scent of the human being behind by letting the scent of the smudge pot seep into our pores.

"Our women prepared the braids of our hair. We were very thorough, wise Kakeokoke."

"And the equipment and weapons that you took, what were they?"

"I carried my medicine bag slung across my chest. It was filled with medicines to lure our prey to us. It also contained my personal items that had given me success in past forays. Finally, I placed in it parched sweet corn, sunflower seeds and my strips of pemmican for energy. Those strips of nuts, berries and fat are so tasty too.

"I also carefully selected my favorite bow and took many sharply chipped and finely tipped arrows with quality tail feathers in my quiver."

"And you honored any animals found and killed by you?"

"I always did that! And if I could, I was there to partake of the slain creature's last breath. I breathed him in fully as he gave up his final exhalation."

Very softly, this marvel of a youth, no more than in his late teens, intoned a chant. Kakeokoke hardly heard the whisper of it but it went like this:

"O Great Spirit, we love, honor and respect you,
And our Mother Earth and strong Eagle as well.
We are part of everything
And everything is a part of us.
We are all one.
Thank you O Great Spirit
For giving us these four legged creatures
To feed and clothe my people.
Today, I am one with you precious animal.
I beg forgiveness from you and
Thank you for your generosity.
Your life has brought my people life.
It is good.
Stay with me until I can come to you
And breathe with you
Your final breath."

"There is no reason then, within our control, that leads me to having an answer for your question. You have fulfilled all. Your hunter's prayer truly does great honor.

"It is something else that makes the animals disappear."

The talk abruptly ceased then.

The parallel of the lessened animals surrounding Cahokia now and the inescapable bleakness of his vision combined cast a shadow over his mind and heart. He shuddered for his culture, his tribe and even himself.

Was there hope?

CHAPTER 34

COPPER'S GLIMPSE

S he found herself reluctant to follow Kakeobuk but chose to be with him in case danger became reality.

"We each see that Mikilenia hid himself and Anteekwa in the shafts of the copper mine. We know that now that he is no longer blocking our seer sight.

"Our discernment would be the very reason that he and she would never return there!"

"My lovely Minkitooni, your logic is impeccable but shallow. It does not reach far enough to sort out the full twists and turns of his diabolical thinking.

"Might he not believe exactly as you propose and thereby find it the ideal location to secrete him and his consort again? He simply blocks our present vision of that area and their doings and imagines that we will never search for them there.

"That is why I must go immediately and find if there is a fresh encampment."

Minkitooni uttered, "Yes my love, you have convinced me. We will check that area together. You may need my help."

It was thick into nightfall. The workshop and mine had been restored but were without artisans working their tables and fires diligently.

The entrance was through the clay hardened, cedar spun door of a mound that was used exclusively for the purposes of serving up copper in its various forms to Cahokia. The workshop became immediate for the two seekers of any undead presence other than their own. They traversed this area, therefore, in short order.

They advanced quickly to the three open shafts that tailed gradually down and away from their present location. The shafts had been dug in the pursuit of finding ever more, and ever more valuable, copper deposits.

With their powerful ability to visualize all details in any shade of black and its kissing cousins, it was simple for them to distinguish all objects, one from the other, and then pick a first shaft to investigate. They swept down the one with the largest opening. Kakeobuk found nothing daunting ever and so he shoved himself onto ledges, around corners, into cracks and crevices and actually anything that might possibly hold bat or human size figures.

Minkitooni did her own scouring of the rough and rocky interior of this shaft, the next tunnel and then the smallest of the manmade holes. There was a complete absence of anything suspicious. They did not even find any remaining traces of Mikilenia and Anteekwa's prior presence.

They were both satisfied that the villain and villainess had departed these premises entirely. They smiled subtly at the notion of how totally dominant Kakeobuk had been over Mikilenia and how he had humiliated the rebel so thoroughly. The irony was that Minkitooni knew how little Kakeobuk had wanted to perform that very act.

As they were about to pass through and then exit the very unique facility that this mound housed for the Indians, Minkitooni took her companion's hand and led him to the cluster of tables where the skilled metal artists worked their magic. She touched a pair of copper earrings, flat hammered and with avian design, beautifully wrought, first. Of all objects within reach, these drew her attention to them the most.

"Aren't these wonderfully crafted my love?" Minkitooni spoke in awe.

She moved to pick them up and hang them upon her ears but Kakeobuk draped his hands over hers and had her replace them where they had originally lain.

He then gently lifted the same two objects to her earlobes and stepped back to study the effect.

"They complement your unearthly splendor so naturally. The gold highlights of the copper catch the radiance of the same colored flecks in your eyes.

"You are perfect.

"I love it as I love you.

"Keep them.

"I will make it up to their maker."

Minkitooni was abashed at his tone and sensitivity; his complements caused her to blush. She went to him then and kissed his lips in a soft, long and lingering fashion.

But lovemaking was not on her mind this instant though she had felt that familiar thrill with him for a moment. She was, however, more entranced by the array of magnificent items on display before her. She flushed in excitement at the skill manifest in the very existence of these objects that were casually strewn upon the table's surfaces. She laughed aloud at the carelessness of these artisans. These men obviously cherished the process and the outcome but were not so attached and attentive to their amazing pieces that they would tenderly and meticulously store them.

In addition to her earrings, and she prized that they were hers, there were copper ear spools and beads of intricate design. There were religious long nosed mini-masks that she was tempted to try on but didn't. She had to understand how all of this was accomplished.

So she asked Kakeobuk, "Tell me love, what is the way here that results in such treasures as these are?"

Kakeobuk was turning a wood handled mace with a massive copper head over and over in his hands as she asked this. "These plates impress me," as he put the weapon down and grasped several very elaborately created small copper sheets formed to appear as a warrior, an eagle or a falcon would.

He gave his attention back to her request of an answer from him.

"Do you notice the three tree stumps with the broad, thick and slightly rounded stones upon them?"

"I do."

"And the embers that still smolder mildly in several pits must draw your sight to them too?"

"Yes they do."

"These pits descend to a level that is greatly sunken and invisible because of the ash that has settled over it. Wood is heaped into these pits, it is then lit and an intense heat is generated. Bars of copper are held within the flames blue and when the metal glows red hot, it is brought to the stones atop the stumps and is then pounded while it cools. This is repeated until it is fashioned as desired.

"So much wood must be used to fuel these furnaces of ours. Many of our people must scour the forests to fetch cut tree after cut tree.

"The resources that it takes to have our copper items and ornaments be produced are endless."

"But well worth it, of course." Minkitooni was sure of that!

CHAPTER 35

A RAW OPAL

Hand in hand, Kakeobuk and Minkitooni exited the copper mine. The night was warm and hazy. This was the time of year when the new antlers of the buck deer push out of their foreheads in coatings of velvety fur. There were noises from the interior of the woods that suggested young bucks were traipsing around showing off those new antlers to their stately does.

From the sky above, the moon glowed and it was painted so pink in color. The light shown down and it cast luminosity not unlike a raw opal. Kakeobuk and Minkitooni strolled to the water's edge and along the terrace of the falls, where the moonlight bounced off the water and it appeared as if rose petals had been strewn about to welcome this pair.

There were others on moonlit strolls of their own; a number of people gathered in an area making music on flute and drum, entertaining one another. Life in Cahokia appeared to be progressing back towards normality. The scars of the flood were receding.

The copper earrings on Minkitooni's ears glimmered against the pink moonbeams and seemed to dance to the sounds of the flute. Kakeobuk held her hand a little tighter and moved a little faster now, to find this couple some much needed seclusion.

The ledge of rock beneath the lowest step of the falls would be a perfect place to hide his love away for a little while. Their footsteps picked up a mild speed and their heartbeats shared a quickened drum beat as they headed toward the falls.

The rushed footsteps of the two stopped abruptly. A tumult of noise from the people was heard behind them. Kakeobuk turned to see what his people were up to. Were they under surveillance this night as he and Minkitooni attempted to steal away?

Following the fingers that pointed to the stars, Kakeobuk's and Minkitooni's eyes gazed upward.

There against the back drop of the oversized soft pink moon, a lone eagle in black silhouette circled slowly. It was highly unusual for the eagle to fly at night, much less circle about here. It was as if the moon called to the eagle to protect the people of Cahokia. At times, it appeared as if the eagle stopped midflight to hover over the light that shown down on the waterfall. Kakeobuk was strangely concerned regarding the lofty eagle's grandeur above them this evening.

The people of Cahokia had a right to be sensing the flight of the eagle as an omen of significance. Kakeobuk's seeing eyes caused his heart to leap and he hastened to have his love soon.

While the onlookers peered up into the night sky still, Kakeobuk stole Minkitooni and placed her onto the ledge and in back of the falls. The rushing of the water would muffle any sounds the lovers might make as they tarried here for a while.

Now, just for this moment, nothing was more important to Kakeobuk than being with Minkitooni. Was it the pink radiance of the moon that found its way through the falls to light up her countenance? Or rather, perhaps it was that she had that glow from within that exuded from every pore of her being. Whatever the truth here, Kakeobuk could not keep himself from taking her face into his hands.

The copper and jewel earrings tinkled as he tipped her chin up to meet his lips. When Minkitooni's lips met his, a simultaneous shiver ran from head to toe of the both of them. Mist from the falls sprayed the couple gently and the miniscule effect at each pore made them shiver all the more.

Kakeobuk reached his cupped hand into the falls and, with the water he retrieved, wet both his hands and began to touch Minkitooni's face. As if in blessing he touched her skin and let the water begin to wash over her. She closed her eyes and received this loving ritual bathing. He continued to cup his hands under the water and moved them down her neck and over her collar bones and shoulders, letting the water warm in his hands then drip down over her skin.

This bathing was very sensual and even more so as Minkitooni continued to keep her eyes closed and allowed her to simply feel everything.

"Remove the top of your sheath, my love and let me cleanse you there," Kakeobuk softly instructed Minkitooni.

She removed the top and her breasts, full and pendulous, began to react to the night air.

"Lean forward a bit, so that I may bathe you now."

Minkitooni leaned forward and her breasts hung freely downward. Kakeobuk had filled both his hands with little cuppings of water and he held one under each nipple. The water began to dribble through his fingers as he opened his hands to embrace each breast. His thumbs glided over each nipple and Minkitooni stood straighter to take his face in her hands so that she could kiss him.

He rolled her nipples in his thumbs and forefingers and she leaned back to raise her breasts to him. In mid kiss, he lowered his head to complete the kiss and add more of the same to her breasts.

His mouth was so tender on her; Minkitooni held his head to her and let the warmth flow through her.

Kakeobuk stood again and resumed the bathing he had begun. Once more his hands cupped and filled with water from the falls which then graced her skin. Minkitooni shivered when his wet hands dripped water over her ribs.

She didn't mind when the water found her toes and feet. She raised her legs one at a time when he caressed the water from her thighs down to her ankles.

But when his hands, wet and filled with water, found her center, Minkitooni was almost startled at the chill that rippled within her. His hands stayed and plied her cushioned flesh; no sooner had she felt the chilling sensation of the water, she felt the heat begin to swell inside her Venus vault.

Minkitooni opened her eyes and reached for Kakeobuk to kiss him more fervently now. She felt the same urgency that was coming upon him. Her hand reached down to caress him and she found that he was so ready for her. Elongated and flaring, hot and heavy in her hand, his cock was dripping with the dew that would help him to slide so easily within her own pearly wetness.

Kakeobuk lowered himself to the ledge of rock and it chilled his back but never once quelled his heat. Minkitooni straddled him and lowered herself down and hovered over him, almost teasing him for a moment. She held him and he held her hips as she guided his cock into her. Once again a perfect fit. The heat inside her was such a contrast to the chill of the water and the night air on her skin.

CHAPTER 36

MAGENA AND TAWA

Kakeobuk's mind felt a sense of urgency at completing this joining, but his heart and his body wanted to take some time and enjoy every sensation with Minkitooni.

There was nothing that could or would happen in Cahokia at this very moment that could be more important than the intimacy with her.

Kakeobuk turned off the clamor in his ears of the people calling out about the hovering eagle. He only desired to hear the sounds of making love with his sublime partner. A bemused smile crossed his face as he was aware that he only sought after her in his eyes, heart, mind, and his touch. Was there anything more?

Minkitooni, above him now, her hands on his chest, slowly moved rhythmically, lifting herself and pushing down against him. Her eyes were closed yet she let every sensation permeate her being. She raised herself up almost to the very tip of him, the flared head nearly out of her. Then she lowered herself, filling her vault with the very length of him, all the way inside her.

"Open your eyes, my sweet love. Let me see your beautiful eyes. Let the pink moon reflect off of them and make them sparkle. Mmmm . . . Yesss. Oh, yesss." The sensations were overtaking him and Kakeobuk was less able to speak for a time. He was enlarging more so and was filling her up as her movements were heating him and creating bubbling lava within him.

Minkitooni opened her eyes and locked with his own. She smiled a tiny smile while concentrating on the growing feelings within her center.

She moved her hands, allowing her palms to rest over his nipples, and at their very middle found the hard pebbles and began the caressing that she knew he loved. Circles, slow and intentional, stirred him and Kakeobuk closed his eyes and groaned.

"Please, keep your eyes open with mine, my love. Let us be so mindful and aware of the pleasure that awaits us soon." Minkitooni kept her slow movements going steadily over his chest.

He growled blissfully as she took his nipples in her fingers and rolled them around. He in turn pulled and twisted on her nipples and she threw her head back a little and moaned. It was pain and pleasure in one note that sang in her breasts. Titillating and drawing, pleasure emanating from their fingers.

He released her nipples and she let them dangle over his own. The touch of nipple to nipple was making it difficult for him to hold back much longer. He loved the torture of the pleasure and the waiting for its culmination.

Minkitooni leaned down to place her lips on his and Kakeobuk received those lips hungrily. She then let her tongue find his. His tongue was more urgent than hers now, dipping in and out of her mouth in rhythm to his cock inside her hot and wet tunnel. She suckled on the tip of his tongue and nearly drove him over the edge!

Kakeobuk drew back and was breathing harder now.

"My love, my release is so close! You are the beauty, the temptress, the woman I so love and desire!"

"Ohhhh, my love, I am reaching that pinnacle soon! Look into my eyes as we reach the crescendo. I want to see your pleasure this night!"

Kakeobuk once again locked eyes with her and took hold of her moving hips. He took the lead now and began to guide her onto him. He moved her up gradually and pulled her harder and faster onto his straining cock. He was at his maximum length and girth, the dew spilling from the flaring plum head as he thrust again and again.

Minkitooni's own rhythm increased as she felt so close to her climax. She moved decisively and firmly, quickening her pace and her breathing. It was becoming increasingly difficult to keep her eyes open but she was determined to absorb Kakeobuk's pleasure through all her senses.

Erotic moonbeams began to build a heat in her ears, eyes and then down her neck. The flame had started and was rushing through her now. She opened her eyes wider and whispered, Please. Please! *Please!"* Minkitooni neared her peak. Her jeweled center was inflamed and aglow from her own fire within.

Kakeobuk, sensing the vibrations that pulsed through her, picked up speed and intensity in his thrusts. His time was near. Oh, his time was *now*!

His eyes opened wide and he groaned loudly, growling as he spurted his hot flowing lava into her. Jet after jet of pearlescent volcanic emission filled her up.

Minkitooni was not far behind as she felt the throbbing thrusts; her own muscles began to clench and pulsate, waves of pleasure rocking her. She thrust herself forward, her face right above his and her eyes peering into his eyes, seeing inside him, his very heart beating in time to her orgasm.

Their hands moved to touch palm to palm and then intertwined fingers as the pulsating continued. This delight was long lasting and they were not about to let it end any time too soon.

He was inside her now and that was where he would stay as they had become one, once again.

Their fit was perfect.

The moon was a lustrous pink. This couple mirrored that very pink from their heart's bounty; the luminous energy came from without and within then.

Nearly out of breath from the intensity of their orgasms, Minkitooni and Kakeobuk reveled in the closeness of their lovemaking. Minkitooni's breasts were pressed against Kakeobuk's chest and she embraced him. She held his face in her hands and kissed him sweetly on his lips from corner to corner. She kissed his eyes. Were those tiny tears that had formed at the outside corners? She kissed them as well, sipping at his saltiness. Her thumbs stroked his cheeks and she quietly hushed, "I love you so," over and over with each taste of him . . . Her eyes welled up and two perfect tear drops fell to his lips. He licked where they had landed, tasting and drinking in her love for him.

It was pure love.

For a time, they had successfully shut off the world outside the waterfall.

However, the calls and cries of the people were getting closer and more persistent. Clanging sounds and thuds of something hitting the ground over and over joined with shouts and exclamations.

"My sweet, sweet Minkitooni, this pleasurable interlude is where I want to stay forever.

"But we must go and inspect and see what the commotion is about. It concerns me. Surely a pink moon and soaring eagle might cause them to worry and wonder but it seems as if more is happening now. Stay by my side."

"I won't leave your side, my love, as that is where I will always long to be."

In their time hidden by the waterfall, Kakeobuk and Minkitooni were completely unaware of what was taking place on the horizon above.

On the night of this pink full moon over Cahokia, the deities, Magena the moon and Tawa the sun were being separated by Mother Earth. The huge bird continued to float in silhouette in front of the night orb.

Earlier, was the eagle trying to warn the people of the anger in the sky?

The people were heard to cry out, "Mother Earth is angry, but look at Magena! She has become angrier yet! Her face is blood red! We must stop Magena!"

The moon was deeply red and rimmed with white flames. Trembling took hold and the people began to throw stones, chanting and calling out for Magena to stop her tantrum.

Women clanged anything metal and began beating wildly on the drums to gain Magena's attention.

Hunters shot arrows into the night sky and more men continued to throw the stones.

Kakeobuk couldn't help but wonder at what the people were doing. The entity had seen it in his incarnations before Kakeobuk. It was, simply, an eclipse of the moon. But the bird might not survive if a rock pounded it or an arrow pierced its flesh.

"Halt!"

Kakeobuk was too late.

But the moon went to pure black then.

Silence fell over the people of Cahokia.

Hearts sank in chests throughout Cahokia. Knees hit the ground simultaneously as weeping and chanting was heard from one end of the city to the other.

Kakeobuk and Minkitooni interlocked fingers and watched wretchedly.

The moon's pure black slowly abated. The anger in the reappearing face of Magena was subsiding and her coloring was returning to its softer pink shade. Mother Earth no longer had to separate Magena and Tawa.

But the eagle had vanished.

The vampires had just witnessed a profound event and even they were afraid.

CHAPTER 37

Recovery Risen

For at least thirty turns of the sun and moon, the land had spoken only peacefully back to the tribe residing on the shores of the massive winding rivers. The damage done at the spring flood's peak had retreated significantly. The once tattered terrain was healing and even thriving in pockets. His people had rebuilt or repaired a majority of their homes. It was a collective process with a syncopated beat that brought happiness to what was now deemed a risen recovery. It was not only the restoration of homes that encouraged the energetic members of his tribe but the fact that familiarity was recaptured. So much had been cleared and then the debris burned, waters had receded so that creeks and streams were recognizable and some very industrious farmers had plowed their soil and the remaining plant debris again so that a quick replanting was possible. These new seeds were to grow stunted and hardly edible but would suffice for a while.

Kakeobuk and Minkitooni surveyed what had been a muddy wreck previously. They were so very proud of the reordering of their now beloved Cahokia without the necessity of submitting to the old traditions. Not a female had been asked nor expected to prostrate themselves before the old gods. And the pair was aware that the one God existent did not demand such.

The entity did not always cherish his master but was ever privy to the knowledge that He was there and watching at all times.

Mikilenia and Anteekwa had not prevailed. Kakeobuk felt that this was permanent. Keokumana Catori was the last sacrificed. There would be no more following.

The tragedy of the accidental deaths of the remaining virgin maidens had been mourned at length. The pain of the incident would always vibrate somewhat, yet the grief would become scabbed over and become dulled thankfully.

This Great Eagle found much softening and contentment within the ever warm essence that was Minkitooni. The proposition of eternal satisfaction was frightening to him; he might find it though within the gentle fanged touch that she invariably presented to him, to all.

They sat cross legged as they scanned the ink soaked horizon.

Minkitooni glanced at her companion and in a hushed tone asked, "Does your brother mention to you his opinion of what has befallen the city?"

"He has, sweet Minkitooni. He is perplexed but less so as tranquility seems to have settled here now.

"And I told him of our experience coming from the falls also.

"I strain to view what the future here portends but my seer sight is peculiarly poor and has been at length. My images are constantly held back by a dense, dark sheet within my brain that is not at all porous.

"Possibly, I have not been practicing my undead powers responsibly.

"I forget to be my demon self when I am around you.

"Often I simply feel boyish and in love." He appeared abashed at this admission.

Minkitooni was blushing radiantly as she absorbed his feelings for her. She returned every bit of his fascination back to him. The round robin of pleasing emotion, the loops of love that spiraled round them and rose infinitely satisfied her absolutely. Her heart beat swiftly; she drew in a quick, short breath and knew that her craving for him was now triggered. Her crown jewel and the flesh surrounding it were suffused with blood and a thick and heavy pulse. Her fount glistened and flowed. And this all because of the fewest of words slow falling from between his lips.

She tucked into him but did not let her insistent desires divert her from probing him deeper than she had managed so far.

"You are my forever, Kakeobuk."

They lingered in this delicious moment. She allowed it to build in tension just short of any point of no return.

Then she abruptly commented, "My vision wanders the wilderness as yours does. It seems that we both must rely on Kakeokoke for the present.

"What further did he discern?"

"He mentioned the death of the mother eagle and the eaglet that did not survive after. He shook his head sadly at that.

"He was overwhelmed when I described the moon's eagle that you and I failed to protect. That bird may have escaped harm yet we will never know. His body was not located but that means very little as he might have flown in fright and injury so far away.

"Kakeokoke has been reassured of late though. The calmness of the earth and the resurrection of the city have relaxed him greatly, to be sure.

"The travels with his shaman ally, the bear, cuts him deepest and remains a definite concern. What he comprehended from that was little but each change of aspect was so vivid! And the final absence of so many was, ultimately, profoundly disconcerting to him.

"He fears it and at the same time does not remotely understand what was presented to him. That so rarely happens when he is guided by the bear."

Kakeobuk peered pleadingly into her eyes and gravely spoke, "How can we save them?!"

"Look to your God my love."

The unknown sorely provoked them both.

CHAPTER 38

MEDICINE MAN

As priest and shaman, Kakeokoke acted in the stead of medicine man additionally. Priest, shaman and Kakeobuk's second were not his only duties.

And what, pray tell, did he have in his medicine arsenal? He believed in all that he did and the implements that he used in his efforts to heal the ailing. They might be ill physically or spiritually; yet he took on all comers and was generally successful in both arenas of health.

He relished all that he did for his people.

This priest, above most all else, cherished his medicine bundle. It was his supple leather bag that carried his secret and sacred items for his use in aiding in the restoration of the health and wellbeing of those who reached out for his skills in their time of travail and uncertainty.

A small boy had come to him and revealed that Kakeokoke's presence had been requested by the family of the boy's father. This father, this hunter, was too pride bound to have made the request himself but his longtime partner and their children were in utmost concern over the appearance of a gash to his leg. So Kakeokoke followed the lead of the young Indian who had come boldly to fetch the medicine man.

As they hurried down the slope of the mound from where he resided, Kakeokoke reviewed all of his tools inside his bundle.

Generally, it contained special roots and specialized herbs with which only he was familiar as to their therapeutic purposes. He possessed paints, spirit objects, fetishes and amulets besides. The amulets were intended to bring the in need person good luck and an auspicious outcome. He took with him small whistles and noise makers to assist in finding a remedy. And though his bundle did not contain this, his chants and songs for the restoration of the victim's strength were every bit as important as the other items in his precious bag.

His special skills in the medicinal arts went beyond what was commonly known. He smiled though as he mentally listed those interventions that were most assuredly already performed by the hunter's loved ones.

Runners and hunters in particular knew the value of taking wild lettuce leaves and roots as a formula for diminishing the power of a snake bite. They rubbed the thick white sap from these same roots on warts and bee stings to limit damage to the sufferer.

Many plants were recognized for their ability to give the predominantly youthful pursuers of all size game lasting endurance and a capacity to trail their prey as necessary. Sunflower seeds and their leaves, evening primrose seeds and their roots and prairie coneflower were eaten along the paths through the forests that they hunted. More substantial foods for nourishment included sun choke and goosefoot. Wild mint, leeks and onions had a capacity to smooth digestion. Not surprisingly, especially the wild onion had a power to drive the insects away from their exposed skin.

Indian parents were also well aware that strawberry leaves left soaking in hot water were able to relieve diarrhea, calm spider and insect bites and quiet skin rashes when the warm liquid was gently washed over the skin surface. Further, raspberry leaves soaked in hot water were very helpful in soothing an upset stomach. A smudge pot burning with goldenrod and dried bee balm leaves assisted with breathing, headaches and colds. Coughs and sore throats were treated with wild cherry bark softened in hot water.

Of this common store of knowledge, Kakeokoke might use the strawberry leaves if he observed any rashes surrounding the wound that he presumed was deep. Possibly he would apply one of his distinctive poultices where the skin was most significantly affected.

They arrived at the hunter's home soon enough.

As he passed through the entryway, he immediately identified the injured brave as the strapping male lying on a pile of furs who was surrounded by one hovering female and several children at a slight distance. They all parted for the medicine man without hesitation.

The stoic father was the picture of blooming health except for the one area of his body that contrasted with his toned skin and rippling muscles. That area was bare and it was his left leg. The gash was very apparent and the surrounding tissue was swollen and red.

Kakeokoke slowly and carefully leaned down to the offending part and examined it closely. As he did this, he asked questions without looking up. He did not want to challenge or frighten this man in any way.

"How did you come by this wound?" Kakeokoke was always very direct in his demeanor as medicine man.

"I was trailing a rapidly moving buck and was using my chest and body to spread the tangles of the forest. I was careless as I drew my weapon to take aim at the animal. A low branch caught in the flesh of my leg. It ripped me and created a jagged pain."

The laceration was of the length of the wide spread space between his thumb and forefinger.

"When did this happen?"

"Several moons ago."

"Be specific. Two cycles, three cycles, what exactly?"

"Three cycles. It was three cycles ago."

Kakeokoke observed the qualities of the wound and felt that he had the requisite skills to provide the cure for this man.

The open portion of the outer calf was no more than a fingernail deep, no blood or pus was oozing from it and the slightly yellowish tinged moist flesh was clean and without abnormalities for this type of injury. There were several tiny black patches that were discernible but they were bruises only, he was sure.

The miniscule pink dots at a level just below the cut were nearly masked by the cut. He almost missed this inconsequential abnormality but saw it at the last moment of close observation. It was nothing and he moved on.

"I also have a tiny area of tenderness at my upper thigh. The skin there is raised and a bit warm."

This information was not important and Kakeokoke dismissed it.

What was important was that he had to cleanse the torn flesh first. The woman had the hot water steeped with strawberry leaves already prepared and the medicine man quickly and expertly washed the entire area of injury.

It took very little for him to lay his poultice over the cleansed area and wrap the wet dressing around the thigh and then he placed a dry dressing over the first. He bound it all with medium tightness and tied off the leather thongs in three locations. A too tight binding would limit the necessary blood flow; a too loose binding would cause the dressing to fall off.

The secret ingredients of his that he had rubbed into the dressings would seep into the wound and give complete recovery.

"You will be well very soon."

The thank you from the hunter was said once. Those from the others, once outside the structure, were profuse and sincere.

CHAPTER 39

EMBRACE AND
DEPARTURE

All four climbed from their automatic slumber on the instant of horizon's darkness. This sleep was profound and revived their flesh so that their energy and hues of appearance were more compelling to humans. Even the contrast of the so pale skin with their depth of color otherwise was utterly alluring.

Therefore, they all arose more beautiful for a while each evening.

Kakeobuk and Minkitooni sought the fresh outdoors with its obsidian shaded skies. Alternately, Mahkwa and Ashkipaki held back. They continued to lounge upon their elevated platform, ensconced among the hides, furs and soft feathered pillows. This was unnecessary excess for one who was undead, yet they luxuriated in it while they had the opportunity.

Mahkwa needed to be sexually sated and immediate entwining with Ashkipaki was how his usual rhythm parsed itself out. This pulse even surpassed his vampire call to his nightly blood feast. Ashkipaki found that, as Mahkwa played upon the instrument that was her body, the flow of her erotic hunger curled over the torment of the belly's hunger and the one perennially swamped the other. And besides, he was her companion whom she genuinely craved pleasing.

It amazed her, and perplexed her, the many emotional similarities between her present species as opposed to the prior species that she had once been long years nigh. Her once human nature did not fall decidedly far from the force of the undead.

So, when Mahkwa turned her upon her back, she was ever prepared for this. She used her shoulders, buttocks and feet then to lift herself and give herself space to untie the thongs at the back of her thin deer hide tunic. She did this fluidly and when it was completely loosened, Mahkwa's eyes danced and shone brightly.

She cherished his feelings for her and whispered to him, "You lead and take all the gorgeous steps from this moment on." Her whispered words aroused him but so did the lovely erotic tickle of her breath upon his inner ear.

"Close your eyes Beauty and do all in your power to be totally still throughout. Can you do that for me, my love?

"Turn your head to the side as well."

She murmured a soft yes and his shaft flared for her. She turned her head away from him gracefully so that her neck fully flashed in his direction. He would tease her though and ignore his erect need for her now.

He let his fangs pierce the skin of her lower nape and brought forth the tiniest rivulet of blood. He licked at it sensuously and then, so that the additional skin remained unbroken, allowed those razor sharp vertical blades of his to float across the continuing span of skin exposed at shoulders and neck. The flesh neither bled nor parted as he skimmed her there.

She moved not; yet her hushed moans and harder breaths gave him clear notice of its stimulating effect upon her.

Her dark braids hung long and the girlish impact of that image stirred his core greatly. His desire for her seemed infinite.

Her chest rose and fell certainly and brought his attention to the tunic that hid her mounds yet. He strummed one of her thick nipples through the thin hide. She felt him play her there and shuddered deliciously.

Her skirt remained in place but his fingers had easy access to her as she wore nothing beneath the tiny garment. He eased three fingers into her opening and stroked her jewel with his thumb, rubbed her wet interior and continued the contact with her nipple's expanding length.

She moaned more heavily now and she was unable to stop her pants of excitement. But she was perfectly without motion otherwise.

He was incapable of waiting any longer. His thick stone hard cock had pushed the hide covering from his groin long ago. His shaft shown long and jerked irregularly in his heated anticipation.

He threw her tunic aside, removed his fingers from her fount and stabbed his length at her gushing vault with an ardor that was explosive. She was still no more and Mahkwa did not care about that a bit!

He bent to kiss her heaving, shaking breasts. To feel the hard pointed tips of her high mounded chest was always thrilling for them both. He pounded her and sucked her lush and firm nipples hard and it took but an instant for the bloom of release to absolutely envelop them both.

A length of time had elapsed before they relaxed into the pleasure of his ejaculation and her orgasm. They almost melted into one another's arms at this point.

"I have not adapted well to this culture, my sweet Mahkwa. I feel invisible and barely of any consequence here. Pictish is still what I am. This community has not convinced me that I am anything but that."

"It is true love; we have become lost in others' shadows. We were never needed and are not needed now.

"It is sad but I am Eumann and my identity remains Gaelic. Eumann and Catrione are who we are."

———

"We will call one another by those names. It is obvious that you relinquish the name Mahkwa and I relinquish the name Ashkipaki as well.

"I love my Catrione."

"Then let us embrace the city once more and then depart."

"I must find Mikilenia too. He can be tamed but only by a mother's hand."

"Very well, my love, I am ready."

He slapped at his ankle's annoyance and then they abruptly left their chamber in Cahokia's principle mound and never looked back there again.

They traversed Cahokia and absorbed its specialness for one last time. They paid quiet homage to the temples on the huge mounds, the vast and finely done playing fields, the wide expanse of the elaborate plazas, the odd set of wooded protrusions designed circularly and plentifully, the barricade that encircled the core of the city, the sweep of new corn fields and, lastly, the monster waters that rushed past the city's margins.

They hoped for Cahokia's perpetual success as they swung up to the limitless dark vista before them and disappeared into its definite clutch.

There was no necessity to inform Kakeobuk or Minkitooni as they already comprehended.

CHAPTER 40

LOVE'S ODE

Ashkipaki and Mahkwa's permanent and unexpected leave taking had engendered, in the entity especially, a mood of pensiveness for Kakeobuk. Profound changes, the sudden loss of loved ones, were the particular subject that he pondered. He viewed his Minkitooni as she reached behind her head to rework one of her beautiful braids. In his mind, she glistened as she fixed what was already perfect. What if he lost her he wondered?

Kakeobuk's heart was suddenly overflowing, like a stream in spring time, with love at the stabbing thought of her absence from him.

And his excruciatingly tender sentiments that washed over his mind regarding her exploded instantly onto the so very receptive canvas that was her soul.

> Minkitooni, my sweet love,
> My heart leaps like a young deer in summer,
> It soars like the eagle overhead,
> It sings like the meadowlark in the early morning,
> It is as gentle as a butterfly landing on a petal of a daisy.
> My beautiful fair one,
> Hair, golden as honey, kissed with strawberry,
> Soft as green silk on the corn.
> My fingers long to disappear in the luster and sheen,
> Entwined in the curls that are soft as baby rabbit's fur.

You are as rare as a pearl
Seldom found in a quahog along the river and
Once discovered, such a cherished treasure
To hold in one's hand.
You are my treasure, my rare pearl.
Your skin compares to the inside of a shell,
Smooth and pearlescent, the blush of pink at the center
Likened to the blush on a peach. I cannot keep from
        touching
The tiny dots on your nose, color of the fawn,
Gifts from kisses planted by sunbeams.
Your eyes, the color of which I had never beheld before,
Remind me of the very eye on the peacock's feather,
Iridescent blue with flecks of brightest green and gold.
The colors dance and sparkle when you look at me the
        way that you do.
I see in them and through them to your very spirit.
Your lips, full and soft, are both touchable and kissable.
I long to touch and kiss them now,
To taste the raspberry that stains them so pink,
To taste the sweetness of your kisses.
The words they form are always music to my ears.
Your lustrous hair, at times, hides the secret of your neck.
My fingers love to trace there and
My lips find their way there,
To kiss the spot that makes you swoon
Into my arms where you so belong.
Your breasts, ahh, my love,
Round and full as melons in late summer,
The pendulous weight of them in my hands, luscious.
The taste of your nipples elongated and firm with
Raspberry sweetness there as well, so delicious on my
        tongue.

My hands find your waist, your hips irresistible,
Your legs long, lean and supple, they call to my hands.
The jewel at your very center, red and shining as a garnet,
I want to kiss and touch.
Even your feet and toes ask for caressing.
All of you, so sensual, my fingers crave you.
I love your curiosity and questions, you make me wonder
     and consider alongside you.
Your equality and fairness, our eyes meet in the middle
     every time.
You have the inner strength and generosity of one born
     with a heart too large
To carry the weight, but you do so wonderfully.
Oh, my Minkitooni, you have captured my heart.
Hold me and never release me.
I never want to leave your loving arms.
I will always hold your love tenderly.
My heart and spirit desire you for always and forever.

His beautiful companion swooned with his unspoken words and he caught her in his arms.

CHAPTER 41

MORE AND MORE

M inkitooni felt the song of love rising in her own heart. The melody of devotion permeated her being throughout and rose softly to her lips as she silently said the words that her spirit wanted her to sing.

My love, my true love, eternal Entity within,
My spirit knows you well
From another time, another place.
Yet my heart feels as if we have never parted.
Let me open my heart to you now
And share with you the bliss that courses through me.

As Kakeobuk, you are the Great Eagle,
Chieftain of Cahokia,
Shepherd of this community
And ruler of this people.
How honored and blessed am I to be chosen by you
And to have you at the very center of my spirit.
Our outward features as seen by others
Appear to be so opposite.
But it is much more than exterior features
That compliments us.
As we join and become one again and again,
Like the flute sounds and the calls of the birds,

We are one harmonizing melody.
Your raven hair, straight as tall grass
And highlighted with blue feathers
Tied with copper rings,
Swings with determination
When you are called to lead your people.
Yet I love how it cascades down your back
When we are alone,
And my fingers comb through the length of it.
It lays over your skin, smooth and tanned
As the pecan shell,
Softer than the deer hide that covers it.
This the skin that lies taut over rippling muscles.
My fingers trace over the mountains in your arms and
        chest.
I tremble for the moments with you
When I lean into your safe harbor.
My fingers and thumbs know so well
The features of your face.
I close my eyes
And I am able to remember in my fingertips
Every nuance of you.
Brows straight and lush, color of soot,
Hover over your deeply set almond eyes
Mink brown, almost coal black,
Shot with lines as grey as
The feather of a mourning dove.
Yet they sparkle with flecks of mica.
Eyes that dart about and scrutinize
When you are serious.
Framed with thick lashes,
Black as liquid pitch,
I meet them when you gaze

Into my own eyes.
Oh, see my chest heave, and hear me sigh
At the very thought of you.
Softly chiseled nose,
Long with concave turn
And nostrils flared
To breathe in the scent of danger
Or the sweet, sweet fragrance of love.
Would that you could enjoy the
Aroma of affection more frequently.
Full lips, ruddy like moist clay.
Strong words released from those lips
To your people,
Like a father who holds his children tightly, though
      lovingly.
Teaching them and calling for them to behave in a better
      manner.
Yet they whisper sweet words in my ear and over my flesh,
Covering my lips and all of me with the most delicious
Of kisses, softer than petals of a day lily.
Softly sculpted chin and neck
Holds your head strong and proud
And calls me to nuzzle there.
Breathing in your scent,
A combination of leather, pine cones, wild thyme, and
      water from the falls,
A fragrance that will never leave my memories.
Your arms, my love, sinewy with such potency in muscles.
And hands ready to fight if necessary.
However, gentle enough to pluck flowers one by one
From the earth for me.
Powerful enough to master me and carry me.
Yet, you hold my hand

And encourage me to walk beside you.
My hands, long to touch your chest.
Tiny nipples so sensitive to touch,
Ruddy as your lips.
Pebbles under my palms.
I love the sound of your excited groan.
Muscular abdomen and back,
I feel so safe with my arms around you.
Sturdy as a silver birch that has lived
Through many moons and storms,
My hands cannot keep from caressing you.
Under your loin cloth,
The treasure you share with me,
The manhood that rises to meet me,
My hand barely holds the girth of you.
Flaring as mushroom, red as the ripe plum,
Earthy salty taste, your dew pearlescent.
You fit me perfectly inside.
I want you to remain in me forever.
The pleasure is exquisite that we share.
But it is the entity that lives within you my only one,
The spirit that I love like no other.
Over time and many years, I have carried the pure
     affection
For the entity, in my heart and my entire being.
This spirit once black and without a home, waiting,
Has found in you a shelter of true compassion and peace.
My eyes well with tears, I need you so.
Do you, sweetest entity within this man, feel the tiny
     openings in the blackness?
Those openings that have let the moon beams shine
     through?

I know in my own spirit that you are not long for this time
and place.
How I love you and want to be with you!
Hold me and let the moonbeams shine onto me and into me.
Then course through me. Never leave me. I love you more
and more.

There was a sense within her that rose to squash her heart. There was to be a parting of the three. Love, after much search, would come to the trio's survivors. The one lost, forever cherished.

CHAPTER 42

RUDE MASTER

Minkitooni, as Aiobheean, had been through this before and so, even though it tore at her heart, she was at least aware of the mechanics of what unfolded before her. She was easily strong enough and she laid her Kakeobuk instantly upon their fur and hide softened bier so that he would not fall and injure himself as Cinaed had.

The Great Eagle had begun to feel an ache in his head which had slowly worsened until he began shivering and then abruptly seized. He was wracked by uncontrollable waves.

The immortal essence was slipping away from him, she knew, and it was a huge loss for her. She loved the harmonious blend. She was not even sure that once they split apart that Kakeobuk would survive this ordeal of his.

As before, she knew equally that she would have to leave her Indian lover and go in search of the one she genuinely cherished. The entity within had been commanded to depart and he had to abide the rude master who forced him to leave his corporeal existence behind. Another skin would be given to him but Minkitooni had no idea of precisely where or when.

There was a shaft of pain that penetrated her emotional being for a moment; and after, she only felt the absence of her love and saw the body which was once possessed now absolutely become Kakeobuk's own.

Yet she also loved the man before her.

This outstanding man, chieftain and moral compass for Cahokia and all who resided within and without the margins of this magnificent city, bled slightly from his bitten tongue but the spasms that had spread from chattering teeth to a shaking torso and then to the wildly irregular movements of his extremities had all but vanished. That was a blessing!

He lay unconscious and oblivious to any touch, word or action of hers. She discerned that it would be this way for a brief period and then he would respond . . . . slowly.

With the entity gone, Minkitooni swept Kakeobuk's mind. She was helpless to do other. It was a reflex that was not preventable and she discovered nothing that would make her want to writhe and shriek as she had when Cinaed had undergone the identical change that Kakeobuk was undergoing right now.

Once he was awake, she was certain of how she needed to give him support and succor in a period of his confusion and bewilderment.

His eyes fluttered subtly and then obviously. He stared in a fixed daze at first and it was as if he were paralyzed.

Minkitooni cradled his head and shifted it so that he was forced to focus upon her face. The smile and warmth that radiated from her seemed to melt the ice that had encased him. He held her gaze and then lifted his fingers to stroke her beautiful and tender features.

He flinched as he noticed her fangs. His shivering began once again; the spasms did not.

"My love, I have much to explain to you." Her gentleness was clear and her concern stark.

"Tell me how you feel first. Can you focus and understand what I am saying?"

He nearly fell off their platform bed because he jerked away from her so rapidly. His grimace told all.

Minkitooni failed to grasp Kakeobuk's terrible fright except that he was still not lucid or able to comprehend what had just occurred. She chose to quell his fears as rapidly and thoroughly as was possible. So she continued her explanation to him. "You are no longer undead my love. The essence that provided you your immortal energy and capacity has vanished from your body. You are human; nothing more, nothing less now!"

He shrank and nearly hissed in her direction.

She moved closer to him in order to offer him a gift that she deeply assumed that he desired from her. Her fangs glittered as she whispered to him, "Let me take blood from you and return you your immortality. It is such a sweet and swift process."

In a fearful rage, Kakeobuk pushed himself off the surface of their bed so that he stood very tall at her side.

She continued to watch his reaction in horror!

"You are Piasa! You are a creature from the bowels of Hell. I know. I remember that I once could fly as a bird can fly. You can do that very thing still.

"The Piasa has come for me. You are that bird monster that reaches for the spirit that keeps me alive and strong. I see your fangs. Your wings and tail are hidden. So is that hideous face of yours that I have never seen but know lurks beneath. I am not fooled.

"You took me once and I was detestable.

"By some miracle I am human again. I will never relinquish that.

"And I cannot understand why I am here in the core of the mound chamber where our people are supposed to be buried. Why am I not in my home atop the highest mound?

"It is evil what you wrought upon me for these long cycles of the moon. But I am free and I am Indian. Cahokia is my home and I am its chieftain. That will never change.

"Be gone monster! Or I will be gone first!"

Kakeobuk backed his way toward the door. He would not remove his focus as he prepared for any imminent attack from her.

Minkitooni was caught off guard and was frozen in place. Her startle over his reaction was primal, shocking and held her rooted. She was unable to speak or move.

She locked eyes with him as he locked eyes with her.

She shuddered as he shuddered.

He blended into the night as he exited in an explosion of speed.

She wiped at her lashes where tears mounted.

If he had lingered any longer, he would have heard her gasping sobs.

CHAPTER 43

BLACK RAIN

Kakeobuk had returned to the lair of the beast. He was the leader of his city and was solely responsible for clearing all nemesis from his chiefdom. It was the bright of day, the first that he had experienced for so long. He luxuriated in the warmth of the sun's rays upon his skin. He was loath to reenter the tomb that he had called home while demented and under another's spell. He had been made mad and it had been sheer madness!

If the she-demon, he never spoke the name Minkitooni ever again, were foolishly still here, she would lie so beautifully in undead repose. He could hardly imagine the concept of a plane existing between life and death but did allow himself the memories of his own enmeshment there to serve him well in the immediate moment. It was a knowledge he had of them and he would use it to purge the world, if need be, of their influence.

He pictured lifting her abominable flesh in his arms, carrying her to the light of day, flinging her from him without hesitation and then watching her burn and disintegrate into the darkness of infinity.

As he had suspected, she was as clever as she was evil, she had departed; long gone.

The cliff painted mural, which had been completed long before he had been born, of the vicious winged Piasa bird was to continue to serve as a warning to the future generations of Cahokia Indians.

The threat had been nearly forgotten and so it had slipped through the crevices by dint of carelessness.

Kakeobuk would see to a continuous future alertness by his perpetual repetition of the message of the bird's potential for deceit and devastation of his people.

As he exited the fibrous and mud plastered door, Kakeokoke was instantly present.

"My revered brother, you are definitely invited to come with me.

"I go to discover the tidings of one whom I nurtured to health recently. He is a warrior and a little thing such as a gash from a limb has certainly been overcome by my poultice and his own healing powers by now.

"I have a disconcerting symptom or two of his that are similar in appearance and in the same location. I want to ask him how he acquired those."

"I will go with you.

"I also want you to know that I am free of my sensitivity to sun's light.

"I walk through sunlight without a care!"

Kakeokoke had been much occupied and it suddenly struck him of the reality of his brother walking side by side with him as the sun shone intensely.

He knelt before his leader and murmured, "You are restored. I am joyous. Forgive me my abysmal inattention."

Kakeobuk raised his sibling up and smiled the issue away. "The oversight is of no concern. I simply am elated that I can accompany you on your trek."

They strode away from the mound to the city's outer perimeter and then to the neighborhood of the briefly weakened, normally valiant, warrior of several days ago.

As they approached nearer and nearer, they heard the faint sound on the wind. The tinged sound that they were able to hear was tremulous and high. The pitch was disconcerting to them both.

Without a word uttered by either of them, they both broke into a run. Their concern was in earnest and they had to find out its source and cause. Was it weeping and wailing that lingered at their ears?

As they charged at full speed through the last of the brush that separated them from the cluster of Indian farmers and warriors homes, they were stunned at the sight and spectacle presented to them. The very putrid odor assaulted their noses and they both slapped hands to nose and mouth to keep from choking on the foul air.

Many bodies lay where they had taken their last breath. The stench was overwhelming and the few who remained alive cried piteously over and over to the gods in heaven . . . if any remained for them.

One such deformed individual crawled as best as she could toward the two men. They stepped away from her in reflex. Her voice quivered and nearly broke as she reached out to them and then wailed, "You must save us. It is you. Our gods have sent saviors!"

She was delirious and she appeared hideous and unclean.

Both the chieftain and his brother were barely able to accept that this once woman was Indian and brethren to them. This was their clan and their people. What black rain had poured down upon their own?

Though Kakeokoke had wanted to flee and never look back, he instead leaned toward the remnants of this woman and asked her to try and concentrate. "What has happened here? Specifically, where is the family of the injured warrior? Think, please. Put your mind to this question and give me some kind of an answer."

The woman swiftly reached out and grasped Kakeokoke at his ankle. Pain flared as she touched him there. It was where he was slightly afflicted; the region of his skin that he had needed to discuss with the warrior. She extended her head up to him with eyes affright and whimpered, "They are all dead. He and his family are all dead. They were the first.

"And then it spread.

"And I know that I will die here along with the others." She placed her cheek in the dust of the ground at this point and rested it upon an arm tucked beneath. She closed her eyes slowly then and let a tiny tear roll off her face and it did not subdue the dust one bit.

Kakeobuk and Kakeokoke were shattered.

CHAPTER 44

ENGULFED BY FLAME

The dream that roused Mahkwa's, aka Eumann's, synapses brought the truth of the matter to him. After this dream, he was never to find daybreak without being securely sealed in material that was impervious to any entry; the lid always perfectly placed.

The disparate images swirled and then came together in a vivid and comprehensible order. And it was as he had experienced the events those many years ago; mostly. And those many years ago amounted to at least one hundred. The streets of London had been dire then.

The dream, in its wild cauldron of horror, stretched beyond the truth only once.

It began with him and Ashkipaki, aka Catrione, vomiting up blood in their revulsion of the mass of fallen bodies strewn casually along the walkways and alleys. And they brought up blood because they had nothing but blood in their bellies. The charnel house that was London and every city in Europe was sickening even to those accustomed to dealing with victims drained and wasted.

The lurid scene shifted abruptly and wavered in the solidity of its picture. He grasped the picture well and good though. His pine box, his retreat upon daylight's approach, had been haphazardly closed in his rush to escape the grimness just witnessed by them both. A slit remained where the lid should have been fully sealed. Into that tiny opening a set of rodents climbed into the black space where he laid. They scurried about and sniffed at his ankles, his armpits and his ears.

The dream telescoped to one of his ankles then. Every microscopic patch of skin and hair follicle was massive. Even larger still was the gigantic pair of fleas that brought their proboscis up from between their legs in order to bore his tender flesh and feed on the rich red blood being pumped so plentifully through the pipes that were a network of capillaries. Their long hind legs, having been used to hop from the rat to the paralyzed man, were at rest now as they took their blood meal.

The fleas were suddenly dwarfed and the rodents became the subject of the uncontrolled journey that his mind was engaged in. The dream's frame of reference twisted and spun for a period and finally settled upon the view of the rodents squeaking and squealing their way out of the pine box. What had scared them away? His leg had tremored harshly and the rats had leapt in a rush.

The horrible reverie tenaciously followed the rodents as they scurried away, up the winding steps, out a seam in the walls joining and onto a path where an ailing woman was leaning against the burnt out lamp post. Her hair hung limply and she moaned repeatedly. Mahkwa felt the insistent pounding of pain against her skull.

The dream afforded him the opportunity to suffer other sensations of hers also.

Her flesh was burning her alive. But the shivering that was caused by the chills of the disease juxtaposed with the sweat that formed all over her body seemed a contradiction. She was being tormented by extremes of temperature and it forced nonsensical words from her mouth. She was delirious. He was in misery as well.

She clutched at her gut and snapped downward so that her vomit flew from her mouth and hit the ground at her feet. How she remained standing was beyond understanding and belief. Wave after wave of pain clawed at her stomach and finally she fell to her knees where her hair dragged in the vomit that she had just spewed. He smelled that putrid odor and would have vomited himself had it not just been a dream in which all, except his mental functions, remained quiescent.

Then she lay upon the alley's surface a while. She finally attempted to roll to her back so that she might use the post of the lamp to give her the support needed to sit up. As she applied all of her mostly wasted muscle in this effort, her bowels blew and the stench of that odor mixed with the other went to his core and nauseated him severely.

She did nothing more from that moment on. She had breathed her last and had expired. This dream was without mellowness or mercy. It revealed clearly the substance and breadth of the reality of an illness that had clamped itself around the human being and had become a nearly worldwide juggernaut. The counting of bodies was lost because so many had died in this sweep of the hand of god over the godless land.

His vision had not ceased. He cowered but was unable to express or show that fright of his.

Was this the end of the world?

It seemed it.

Again the shifting of position within this nightmare occurred. He was not capable of calling it a dream anymore.

He had sight of the woman from four corners above as if he were squared and omnipresent.

He was guided to several lumps at her groin. The invisible force of this impossible set of imaginings pushed his head toward her vile smelling crotch. With this closer view, he winced, though he actually did not, as he was made to observe the many boils that had exploded open and were now simple, irredeemable craters of the deepest sort surrounding the few remaining lumps.

He was whipped from her groin to her armpits where he witnessed the very same characteristics that he had just observed on her fleshy terrain below.

He was returned to that omnipresent position.

All was without sound. His mind registered absolute silence.

Then there was a blurring and the scene was pitched into a foggy motion.

He was oh so weary of all of this.

His weariness was of no concern to his mind.

With the dream's one exaggeration, the woman burst into flame when he least expected anything to happen. It engulfed her and she was no more. She was wiped out and removed.

She was annihilated.

Clouds appeared without end. He comprehended the wind against his beating wings and he flew into the pinpoint blackness that was the end of his dream.

But it was not. The tiny black dot expanded and he was in a different land with his partner and ever lover.

The irony was that it took a flight of mind to reveal the reality that had once shown itself to his very wide awake eyes.

CHAPTER 45

SUFFERING ENTITY

The breadth and depth of his latest retreat intrigued him more than any prior retreats of his. He had shapelessly skied from the land of the trisecting rivers about fifty years ago and was yet in the midst of exploring the cavernous hole where he presently rested.

He was well provided for as there was abundant blood at his disposal with much wildlife roaming the perimeter of this cave's opening. The overhang of rock at this opening managed to keep the light out effectively if nestled a ways back. The entity was even further back than that. The stream that flowed along its floor was easy and mild. He had no practical use for it, as he had no practical use for the salt deposits, stalactites and stalagmites that pocked the surfaces. The sound of the flowing stream at least soothed him when he required that.

This stone tunnel that he was ensconced in had carved itself underground beneath the mild peaks and thick forests of the Smoky Mountains.

The entity loathed his formless condition but was powerless in the face of the insistent dictates of his misbegotten master. The entity suffered again the eventual command to inhabit another skin. How long would his invisible overlord take this time?

The years between habitations had shortened with each new episode of his human invasions. The assaults on the body and psyche of these individuals of significance reinvigorated the entity thoroughly. These adventures were what he craved. His sadness upon the inevitable departure was extreme and always a crisis for a time.

For now, as the black energetic mass that merged with shadows and darkness, he eventually occupied these periods with a bit of fixation regarding the individual that he had last been. He was only able to do this once his seemingly bottomless sadness had passed. The difficulty of reconnecting prematurely was utterly debilitating.

The sadness had passed. So he let his seer sight drift to Cahokia along the Mississippi.

He played a game with himself in order to soften any blows that might come his way from a look-see into the outcome of all involved. The game served as a buffer. He did not have to immediately view the grim aspects that might cut into him deeply. His tenderness surprised him completely.

Before he wrestled complete control over his journey, two pictures coated his mind. One was of an emptiness of the land he had wandered as Kakeobuk. The other was the arrival of a band of European sailors to the coastline of this country; though still many miles from Cahokia itself.

So he comprehended that Cahokia had not survived.

His heart cracked at this but did not break. He mustn't delay forever so he went forward with his game in spite of the awful news.

What then had caused this and what of the citizens that he had ruled, the friends that he had acquired and his brother most definitely?

He continued his mental game and instantly went to the surmise of Cahokia's demise. That came first because it hurt least. It was general and not personal.

Was it the natural disasters that might have occurred after his ungracious exit?

The flood had come and the city had been rebuilt. It was not the flood.

Any drought had been dealt with and the people had overcome those attacks that parched the land. It was not any drought.

Tornadoes ripped structures apart but those structures were always rebuilt. It was not a tornado.

Fires rushed through the city often enough but again the resilient people survived and restored the city to its prior glory. It was not one fire or many fires.

Snow was rarely of such magnitude that it had any permanent impact. It melted and little to no damage was done. It was not snow.

He detected that of all possibilities of natural disaster, earthquakes might be the most lethal. Not only were structures ruined but leaders were often swallowed up by the gashes in the earth that opened up. Without leaders, disorganization and failed restoration followed. But if this had contributed, and he discerned only a possibility of this, it had not contributed in a primary manner. He scanned the land and observed no land gashes significant enough to have had the catastrophic effects required to bring down this mighty city.

Natural disaster was not the source of the vanishing of Cahokia.

He knew of the one and only God, his Master. It was not the cessation of virginal maiden sacrifice to the gods as those gods were nonexistent.

Had the city finally overwhelmed the natural resources of the area? There had been much cutting of wood for cook fires and fires just for warmth. Their shelters, temples and their massive palisades that encircled the core of the city used a huge amount of this resource. As the numbers mounted in that once lush land the need for wood was stretched even further. Certainly this was a factor; but not the predominant one.

He visualized other resources being taxed as the numbers of people swelled. Excessive hunting limited the animals available for meat and the making of hides for clothing. Again, he surmised that this was only a portion of the reason for the disaster that Cahokia had become.

The land itself had been overplanted with maize. Indian farmers had not allowed the fields to be fallow or rotated in order to reestablish their quality; minerals were leached from the soil and nothing grew as swiftly or as proudly as before. No, not the vital reason the entity comprehended.

Lastly, almost, he circled around the idea that the overall climate itself had fundamentally changed. Had it? Had it become consistently warmer or colder? Was either enough to devastate a land as full of abundance and vitality as Cahokia had been? His superb instincts told him no.

He came to the final reason. He had purposely delayed the thought of it as he understood it to be the reason for the Indian's capitulation and elimination from the land. And in going to this event, he had to confront the personal.

Here it came. He yielded to it and kept strength so as not to be overwhelmed.

The contagion had been brought by Mahkwa he now discerned. He had not figured that out then as he had his focus on so much else.

The contagion had followed Mahkwa from Europe to the new continent. The rodents established it; the fleas passed it along and by Mahkwa's flea bites he carried it. How had he done this? The fleas fed on his vampire's blood and it gave those fleas the same immortality that Mahkwa had. The insects did not die in their normal cycle now. They stayed with Mahkwa in perpetuity. With this invincibility, they rode his ankle for over a hundred years and all the way to the new land. Some fled him and found hosts that were merely human and vulnerable to the disease's effects. The contagion was seeded and Cahokia was to be its utter victim.

Both Kakeobuk and Kakeokoke died a wasting death. It was grisly and the entity felt it profoundly. The shaman's trek was answered. The flame of disease had struck.

No person escaped the swath that the Black Plague created. Yersinia Pestis was lethal beyond control.

The land was only to be revived by new people.

The mounds remained and loomed large. They would survive at length he knew.